NOTHING I$ SACRED

The sizzling sequel to *STREET GENERALS*

BY

BOOG DENIRO

Printed in the United States of America

ISBN: 978-0-9828144-1-3

Cover Design: Onine Jennett for S.G. Publishing

Editing: Jacqueline Denise for S.G. Publishing

Typesetting: Carla M. Dean, U Can Mark My Word

Published by:
S.G. PUBLISHING
THE BRONX, NEW YORK
sgpublishingllc@gmail.com

ACKNOWLEDGEMENTS

Once again, I've completed a work of fiction. My third novel, which I thoroughly enjoyed piecing together. And I have my imagination to thank. And of course some other people. My moms; I love you. Naquan, thank you so much for being your brother's keeper. Love you sis. O-Nine, Coo of S.G. Publishing, it's a good thing we put a value on ourselves instead of letting someone else do it for us. Love you, my nigga. Pauline, you never cease to amaze me. Nicole, in a perfect world…you already know. Love you girl! The immediate fam: Sade, TY, Malik, Raheem, Sha, Dell, Zahir, Zoey, Cyann! Love ya!

Can't forget the readers, my fans, the vendors, the retailers, the stores, media markets. Black Star Music & Video, Urban Legends Book Store, Why Magazine, UBO Newsletter. Shout out to Alina Johnson. You're everything that should be expected of a lady. Shout out to Antoine "Inch" Thomas and the whole movement. Thanks for the support, bee. Word up! Shout out to my AMG brovas! Cat, Dutch, Buddah from 240, to name a few. Shout out to the S.G. Publishing crew: Killa, China, Young World, Bugsy aka Rab, Myles "Dutch" Ramzee. My editor, Jacqueline Denise. My new PR, Christina Layden

Before I start forgetting people. Calvin T. Posey, Johnnie "MANN" Witherspoon, Ted Citi, Al Duran, Scott Penn, Daniel Castro, Tankhead Janel, Yo Nitti, Ty Gunz, C-Gutta, Mac Boney, Dominican Jose, Roc Wells, General Jafar Saidi, Mook Young, Streets, Chico, White, Rome Henry, Blacko Macko, Roscoe McClary, Terrence Brisbon of Contagious Art Gallery, and my dude DeShante Lewis – get in that law library! Shout to all my niggas from the Bronx, Stacktown, BK, Southside Jamaica! My niggas from Baltimore, York, Philly, N.C. and the Burgh!

Rest in peace to my fallen komardes. The family members who are no longer, you live through me.

My women friends! Fancy Cat, Luscious Lips, Sheba, Shaunny Charisma, Angelique, Diamond, Becca! Don't lighten up, tighten up!

My barber, Mo Sippa! Thanx for keeping me sharp! You got a long and bright future ahead of you bee. And, Romello, holla at ya boy! You put me on the cover of your first magazine! That is sacred!!!

Never take for granted what can be taken from you any time.

NOTHING I$ SACRED

ONE

All morning Capri had been cruising the city and smoking blunts, basically numbing his pain. There was still no leads on Action's whereabouts and Daffany wouldn't stop blowing his pager up. Patience could see the difference in her man since the last time they were together. Could tell something was eating him alive. But no matter how many times she asked him, "What's wrong?" she would get the same response. "Ain't shit, I'm good."

The conflicted demeanor had her lost, confused, and uneasy. Never before had there been a time Capri couldn't confide in her. This she knew. And what pained her most was he wouldn't even look her way. Clothed or nude she was as pretty as the city's skyline at night. Bright hazel eyes, glowing skin, flowing hair. This summer noon, she wore her best ensemble an Ellen Tracy design the color of ripe peaches that fit her frame perfectly. Shoes to die for. Accessories she made look good.

Three quarter of her legs were exposed, just for him. Toes attended to, just for him. Cleavage on display, just for him. No panties…just for him. But, for him, the reason he couldn't give her his piercing eyes—the guilt knowing she'd been slighted, robbed of the right to birth his firstborn. That was causing him great distress. And the facts surrounding Olivia's death just added a deeper and darker degree of havoc to his decadent life. And for the first time he felt no comfort in her company. The last time he was this hazy, Patience lost him for a year. To steel gates, barb wires, inconvenience and ridiculous regulations.

Since he wouldn't talk she enveloped herself in Mary's melody, glared out the window, and marveled the Harlem streets that corrupted him.

"You ever think about just getting away from here, Pri?"

"Never."

For her viewing pleasure was debauchery at its worst. It was almost as if she could see the grim reaper floating, souls roaring with civil wars, and couldn't help but wonder was she the cause of Capri denying her so vehemently. Being reduced to his accountant was something she couldn't fathom, but that's the way it was looking, the way it was feeling.

Before asking to be dropped off, Patience took one last stab at puncturing the thickening tension. "Pri, what is going on with you?"

"Ain't shit."

"You came and got me two hours ago, and the only time you looked at me was when you said, 'P, this a hundred thousand...put this in the house.' What the fuck is up with you?"

"I'm good."

"If you really good, you doing a bad job concealing your little fucking attitude. And right now I'm not feeling you!"

"P, you buggin," he countered, wishing things were different, wishing life was still so simple. "I ain't got nothing to hide, nothing to prove."

"Then look at me," she demanded before snatching his right hand from the steering wheel, "when I'm talking to you!"

Reacting quickly, Capri grabbed the wheel with his left hand. "Fuck is you doing?"

"Trying to get your attention!"

Capri glared at her through squinted eyes, "Act right!"

"Act right? Man take me home! I didn't know spending time together meant riding up and down Fredrick Douglas Boulevard! Who the hell are you looking for?"

"None of ya --! Told you before don't ask things you don't wanna know!"

"None of my business? I wasn't like that when ya ass was locked up! Ya business was mines when I was accepting the collect calls! Putting you through three-ways, and keepin' ya commissary fat!"

"Nah, I know you ain't go there. Bitch, you ain't do nothin' for me I wouldn't a done for you!"

"I'm sooorry, I didn't mean it to come out the way it did."

"Don't touch me!" he flipped, as he pulled his arm from her grip.

She removed her Gabanna shades from her eyes and tried piercing his skin with an intense stare. And at that moment she couldn't stand him. He had become the boyfriend she could no longer count on. "Take me home!"

"You sure you wanna go home, P?"

"I said take me home!" she screamed.

The next cab base in sight, he pulled over, got out and employed a livery woman to transport Patience home. The driver pocketed the cash, and Capri walked over to the other side of the Hummer. He pulled the passenger door open, and calmly stated, "Come on! You wan' go home? She gon' drop you off!"

Patience's face became distorted, and then the drama ensued. "Nigga, is you crazy?? I ain't takin' no fuckin' cab! You takin' me home!"

He knew his problem wasn't her, and she shouldn't have been exposed to his chaotic affairs, so he said, "You're right," got in and took her home.

During the ride back to Y.O., the silence continued. For Pri, the things that needed venting held no pertinence with her. He thought, 'Only if the right words would come to me, I wouldn't be so stressed!' It bothered him to see that his recklessness had her discombobulated. But...it was what it was.

When he slowed up in front of her home, he noticed a lot of

stirring, a lot of activity. There were a few men garbed in black FBI issued jackets, backing in and out the house. And the only color man was Trent, Patience's father.

"Yo, I though you told me ya pops don't be here no more?!"

"What?"

"My fucking money is up there!"

"My dad don't give a fuck about your money! And he don't be here like that!"

"Ayyo, P...you buggin', shorty? Get it right!"

"Shorty? Get it right?" she uttered.

Patience was convinced she was losing him and he was losing his mind. So without reply, she got out and flung the door shut. Even in heels, her feet were vastly moving with forward progress, never looking back. Frustrated, he closed his eyes and pounced his head back against the headrest. When he opened them, he slammed on the gas pedal. The truck skirted out, but before he caught speed, he was flagged down by a brown skin brother with wavy hair, a six foot stature, and a 5 o'clock shadow on his beard.

What the fuck this dude want? Pri asked himself as he pumped the brakes, then backed up. He let the window down to see what the verdict was, but Patience's pops said, "Pull over, we need to talk."

Adhering to the command, Capri complied, and the government official climbed in.

"What up, Mr. Trent?"

Before speaking, he looked around. "This is a nice truck, and that's some good ass weed. Can tell by the aroma. You know they use these in the military? Yours or did you take it?"

"I borrowed it," Capri sternly replied.

"Come on, I keep it real with you. Keep it real with me, Capricious," sneered the federal agent, as he leaned the passenger seat back to his liking. "I think we both know and respect each other enough to tell it how it is. I call a ball a ball, and a strike a strike. And you know this man."

"I told you, my homie let me push this. Now do a nigga need a lawyer for us to keep rappin'?"

"Cut the cavalier shit! We better than that! So, I'ma lay it all out for you. Since your resurgence from prison, there's been a lot of murders uptown. Donneray Williams was killed, and left in the morgue on a damn block of ice! The same night, your former robbery accuser, Monte Montanez was murdered. The shells were discharged from the same gun! The next night a mother, her son, and sonny Sanchez were found in pools of blood! Sonny was Action's fuckboy, and the third victim in that triple homicide, home invasion. So, if I wanted you, you wouldn't be running up in my house or my goddamn daughter!"

"I feel you, and I heard about the casualties. But I don't know nothin'."

"I'm not saying you did any of this, but I know you know something! And I'm tellin' you, I've been assigned to a special agent's team located in Harlem's three-two precinct. That's your stomping grounds. And your name is under the scope already! There's too many unsolved murders and kidnappings in Harlem, and the government has stepped in. we've already determined Action to be at the helm of it all. And if the bodies ain't droppin' in the hood, the lifeless corpses were residents of the 10039 zip code! So, whoever wanted them dead either killed them in Harlem and took the bodies to the Bronx, or had them executed up there. Look, I'm giving you a heads up, on the strength of my daughter."

The information stunned Capri. Trent was a standup nigga with pure street smarts, so Pri knew he had no reason to pull his chain, and what he was saying had validity. "Who else you got under the radar, and what y'all investigating me for?"

"Marcel Pierce Junior, Savon Hayward, Anwar "Action The Voice" Outen…and Joseph Abraham, Action's right hand man. And you're affiliated with them all, one way or another!"

Stink, Zest, Action, Brother Joe…Capri thought avoiding Trent's green eyes.

"Tiger got your tongue, Capricious?"

"I don't know what you talking about," Pri abruptly stated, his sight set on the steering wheel.

But the agent wasn't trying to hear that. Trent was too familiar with Capri's tumultuous lifestyle. "See, I'm try'na look out for ya ass, and you try'na play me! Savon is your cousin! Known as Zest in the streets. And I can put you both at the double homicide in the Yonkers Ave grocery store back in '89. Yeah, I thought that would getcha attention."

"I was locked up in '89!" stammered Capri.

"The biker! And you were home, on furlough or some shit! Now moving on! Marcel goes by Stink! He's supplying Harlem's elite with tagged foreign cars that he's shippin' from Massachusetts! That's who let you hold this! Pri, I'm the Feds, and somebody's going to jail...if the killing doesn't stop! It doesn't have to be you..."

"What?" Capri snapped. "I'm a G, I ain't no fuckin' rat!"

"Pump your brakes, and stop speeding!" Trent insisted as he slid his hand over the nape of Capri's neck, looking at him the way an irate father would a stubborn son. "I don't want you to turn snitch! I want you to throw me a bone every now and then."

"If I throw you a bone, it ain't gon' have no meat on it!" Capri replied in a tone that left no room for misinterpretation.

"You ma'fuckas could be operating without government interference, if the killing stops! Free enterprise. You think I don't know that you're heavy in that Blood thing?"

"Okay, but—"

"I also know you're respected out there."

"—What that mean?"

"And I know Action's your main man, that he's got don status, and how he makes his living. Bleeding the community. That knowledge alone can get you booked on domestic terrorism. That's what that means."

"Domestic what?" Capri quipped, having never heard of the

federal charge.

"Terrorism," Trent lamented. "Trespassing and vandalism is where it starts. Sticking your hand in the pocket that doesn't belong to you, your nose in business that isn't yours. Rallies. Things of that nature are domestic terrorism."

"Bullshit!"

"Real shit! You're added to a watch list, and by the time we're finished surveilling, we've got enough for a CCE indictment. And before we even deal or ask for a proffer, cats are rolling over on their mothers!" Trent paused, peered over at his pals, the cats he'd be working the Harlem probe with, watched as they loaded the last of his office supplies onto the trunk of the jet Crown Vic. "Like I said, it doesn't have to be you. I'd rather be back in VA on some bullshit detail than the city."

"I can't help you."

Roughly the same height, Capri and Trent's eyes locked, Trent's hands now back at his sides. There was no wavering from either man, and no question the Feds were close, too close. And precision would be detriment if Capri was to avenge his mother's death, and get away with it. Both men had big egos, Twin Towers big, so neither was budging.

An outlaw with the potential to become an in-law, thought Trent as he reached for the door handle shaking his head. "I warned you," he said unable to predict how this would end, and wondering how it all began...

It was a dense autumn afternoon when his wife had noticed the sudden change in their daughter. Trent was watching an NFC East showdown between the New York Giants and the Philadelphia Eagles when Mary sauntered into the den, pasta sauce smearing her apron, and a look of concern plastering her face. Disturbing his focus, she said, "Patience isn't here yet, and dinner is ready. Third time this week."

"She can't be far," Trent shot back never removing his eyes from the television screen.

15

"The last time she was late she was down at the park with Pearl Hayward's nephew," Mary returned positioning herself in front of the wide screen. "I don't like it, babe."

Trent didn't know what to expect when he got down to the park, nor did he know much about the Hayward kid, but by the look on his wife's face he knew there was nowhere more important to be down at the park. He took one last peek at the game before escaping Mary's steady eyes.

When he got to the park his thirteen year old daughter was cheering on a pure shooter with a lanky frame, jet curly hair, and a high yellow hue. The rim was line an ocean, and all Trent could hear was "swish!," Patience beneath the net securing rebounds. The kid couldn't miss. 15 footers. 18 footers. A quick flush off a vertical hop that looked so easy Trent wanted to see it again. And almost as though Capri could read the man's mind, he did it again. This time with both hands.

As Trent watched from a distance, the sun fading to black behind him, he smiled deeply. Never before had he seen such brilliant talent up close, or so much joy on his daughter's face. But what he remembered most about that day was the two teens kissing—his baby girl being the initiator—and him never saying anything about it. Probably because he didn't see a kid with his tongue down his daughter throat. But instead, a potential recruit for Kentucky, Kansas, Duke, or North Carolina, playing on national television every weekend before eventually becoming a lottery pick.

Little did he know, that one selfish act would have continuing ramifications for years to come.

By 1989 Capri was allowed in their house, though Trent thought fifteen was too young for his daughter to be in a relationship that already had a life span two years. Trent remembered Mary saying, "As long as I can see what's going on." And he thought, what about what we can't see???, that kiss of years ago in mind.

Like Patience's body, seasons changed, and so did Capri's

demeanor. When he wasn't at their home, Trent found himself worrying. And when Capri was there, Trent wanted the kid gone. Not only did Capri not go to college to play ball, as Trent secretly hoped, but the only reason he even finished high school was because of family court. Each time Capri went to juvenile lockup, he excelled academically. So much that every time he was released he'd be so far ahead of his peers in public school, guidance counselors had no choice but to promote the criminally depraved truant to his respected grade. And his final year he was able to avoid trouble long enough to finish school as one of High School's top scorers in New York State. Scholarships were in place. Agents were calling off the hook. Sports writers were publishing articles about him. He had even shined at the 1992 McDonalds All-star Game. And just when Trent thought Capri was on the right track, and going places, Capri was picked up leaving the famed Skate Key on murder charges. Capri spent the night in the Tombs, two weeks on the boat, and ten months on Rikers before eventually being acquitted of all charges. Through that whole process Patience stood by him. And all Trent could do was watch, wondering "What if."

Now he couldn't get rid of him

Or could he?

"So, how are things between you and Patience?" Trent asked half his body in the Hummer, half out.

Capri said, "It's been nine years. And we're still going strong."

The sarcasm didn't fall on deaf ears. "Then why she storm off like that?'

"Why don't you ask her?"

Trent nodded then walked off hoping his daughter had finally come to her damn sense.

Capri nodded back the sped off, Harlem the destination, with Zest on one line and Stink on the other. "Meet me at Wilson's. I gotta put something in y'all ear, and something in

17

my stomach."

Neither man asked questions, the urgency in Capri's voice evident, and was there when Capri stalked in. he was escorted by the hostess to their table, a perplex look on his face. The Black owned restaurant wasn't crowded, but it was far from empty. Capri passed a group of women in their church hats humming hymns and gossiping over swine and grits. A few couples candoodling over late breakfasts. Graying old men ogling the scads of scantily clad working girls scattered about trying to fill their tanks. And there was Stink, leaned back like the Mack, high out his mind. Zest was right across from him, phone to his face.

Before taking his seat, Capri gave them both dap, then said, "I didn't expect it to be this crowed."

Stink said, "It ain't that bad. What's poppin' though?"

"The Feds looking at us," Capri informed them just above a whisper, his eyes all over the place.

"What?" Stink shrieked bring the unwanted attention Capri had hoped to avoid.

"Huh?!" Sext huffed, hand over the receiver of his c-phone.

With their brows raised and ears wide open, Capri laid it out just the way it had been given to him. Even though the inside information had come from Patience's pops, Capri felt funny repeating it. His gangsta has never been in question, but the way Stink was looking at him wasn't exactly validating either. As if Capri didn't already have enough shit on his plate. A baby on the way by a dame other than Patience. Then there was Shyann and her threats of dropping dime on that triple murder if she didn't start getting the dick. And then the task of getting to Action before the feds did.

Flaming, Capri said, "My name ain't never been associated with nothing but G shit. So don't give me that look."

Stink knew he was wrong, but one could never be too sure. In the 90s alone he'd seen quite a few cats cave under pressure. "He mentioned Massachusetts and my government?"

"Straight like that," Capri made clear. "And Zest, the nigga mentioned the biker from Yonkers Ave,"

"They didn't follow you here, did they?" asked Stink, peeking out onto Amsterdam Avenue through the window they were seated by. He'd never seen the inside of a prison and had no plans to.

"What type of question is that, bee?" Capri snapped. "You in violation, Stink."

"That wasn't even a question, that was an insult," Zest added in his raspy baritone.

"The kind any nigga in his right mind would ask if presented with some shit like this," Stink replied in his defense. "Them ma'fuckas might be somewhere try'na take our pictures."

"He just told you the source is wifey's pops," Zest seethed across the table.

"Fuck out of here, Zest!" Sink sneered.

"Both of y'all niggas be easy," Capri insisted, his powerful aura reappearing for the first time since entering the restaurant. "We good though, if the murders stop."

"Easier said than done," Zest said, then told whoever he was on the phone with, "We're moving on with that. Peace."

Eyes wavering between the two cousins, Stink said, "What murders?" He wasn't sure if Capri was referring to the body up in Soundview, that had been disposed of expertly, or some other shit. But he wanted answers, some sense of security.

Capri said, "Murders period."

"Pri, It's too late for that. The pens have been lifted, and the ink is dry. He gotta go, but first she gotta go."

"What's poppin' Blood?' Stink quizzed, scooting up in his chair, elbows on the table, eyes all over Capri.

But a top heavy waitress with big brown eyes and long legs sauntered over, halting Capri response, her attention rapt on Stink, the gold in his grill, the Rolex on his wrist, likening the young Blood to some flashy rap star. As soon as she was done

"You left that morning with thirty thousand, and when you came back you didn't have it. I checked your pockets while you were showering."

Naturally, Capri became suspicions. Thought maybe, for a split second, just a split second, that Trent had flipped his own daughter. That they may've been being recorded. Then that inkling of distrust or the lack thereof was obliterated when Patience said, "I also remember you fucking me like I'd never been fucked before. So good, I still don't know if it was passion or anger that made you leave me with that cocky bowlegged stance."

After hearing a few more of her choice words, he realized she was wild drunk. Hit him she slurred, "Remember, remember when, when we got arrested in Harlem, and and I said the gun was mine. There isn't another nigga on this planet I'da did that for."

"Patience, you been drinking?"

"You make me drink, Capri. Sometimes I don't hear from you for days, sometimes weeks. I don't know if you're dead, or back in jail. And as of lately, I just don't know what's going on. Yes, I had a few glasses of wine. And, I'm gonna pour some on your dick and suck it off when you get here. Was gonna wait until your 23rd birthday next week, but Mommy and Daddy's gone now."

"I'm not coming to Yonkers." Capri replied, making his first attempt at the hefty plate of fired food before him.

Patience release a series of restless sighs full of unspoken words, creating this eerie air between them. Capri could hear Neo Soul's Maxwell crooning in the background over her heavy breathing.

"Patience?"

"I thought it was that phone call, but now I'm convinced it's another chick. Has to be," she said, revving up. "You've been trying to get me to give you head for five now, and when I finally decide I'm ready, you tell me you're not coming. I bet' not find out who this bitch is, because if I do, I'm put a cut on her fucking face to match yours!"

Click!

Capri sat his fork down, tried getting her back on the phone. But it went straight to voicemail. He called the crib and the answering machine picked up. As he finished off his home fires, sunny side ups, and fired fish, he thought of Christine and the stomach that would be protruding her sexy chocolate body very soon. Hoped she and Patience never bumped heads. Reflected on the threatening words of Shyann. Then came the inevitable; avenging his mother's death. 'Six Million ways to die, choose one!' he imaged telling Action, knew in his chest, gun to his throat. Then he thought 'Something of this magnitude deserves originality!' before coming to the conclusion that the whole thought was silly, and that the only thing that mattered was that he take his last breath. And soon.

"What's up? You sittin' over there in a zone," Zest said to Capri, surprised by how fast Capri cleared his plate.

"I need a cigarette," replied Capri, stretching and yawning.

"You don't even smoke cigarettes," Zest snickered. "None of us right here do. So what's up?"

Capri finished off his iced tea, then said, "Wifey. If I don't get my act together, I'ma lose the best thing to ever happen to me. And right now I don't see her in my future."

"Well you had better, because we need that inside information," Zest shot across the table in a low and discreet pitch that only they could hear. "We got a lot of unfinished business."

Stink said, "I'ma tell you like Rosa told me: There are people who take things one moment at a time, and there's people who live in the moment. Living in the moment you string bunches of moments together long enough that you end up with chains of events—events that shape your life for years to come."

"Well most of moments and events haven't been with her

lately. And with the way things been shaping out in the last week, things could get worse before they get better. A baby on the way, fed on the scene, and making old school pay."

"Baby on the way?" Stink asked.

Capri nodded, preparing to take care of the tab. "Yeah, got the other woman pregnant. All this at one time."

"Lil' mama from Eighth Ave?"

Again Capri nodded. "And though her father killed my parents, I'm happy she's carrying my seed."

"Run this by me again?!" Stink begged.

Capri tried explaining the back story without it sounding so much like a soap opera script it seemingly resembled.

Action was bangin' my moms and Christine's moms at the same time. Got Mecca pregnant the threatened her he'd kill her if she told anybody, before cutting her off for a life with my mother. But when Action found out the only child my mother had given birth to years earlier wasn't his son, he had my true father killed, then a couple years later off'd my moms, then went on with his life thinking this deep rooted murder plot built on heartbreak and hated would forever remain a mystery.

The only thing that puzzled Capri was the place in which she was killed. As far as he knew Action had a slaughter hose. So why kill her in the projects in which she was born and raised?

Stink ran his hand over his cornrows, then over his full stomach, then consulted his watch. "That's some real ill shit, bee. Listen, I got a boardroom meeting in twenty minutes."

"A board meeting?" Zest quipped checking Stink out. He may've not cared much for the kid, but he damn sure respected Stink's function, and believed that anybody had potential to rise above the malevolence of Harlem, it would be Stink.

Stink grinned, loving the fact that Zest was loving his style. He smoothed down his Polo rugby and said, "Yeah, once a week. I'ma let my boys know I'm shuttin' shit down in Mass, and putting them back in tow trucks. It's gonna cut into revenue. But fuck it, feds ain't trappin' my body."

"Tow trucks?" quizzed Capri.

"Yeah, random repossessions. That's how I got started. Before we found a way to take 'em off the lots brand new, we were hooking nigga's shit right up to pickups, repainting them then putting them right back on the streets."

"So y'all fronted like y'all was repo niggas?" Zest asked, bugging and thinking of what he'da done if some cat with gold fronts, gold chain, and red faced Rolexes tried to repossess his vehicle.

With that shrew grin on his face, Stink nodded.

All Zest could do was smile back at that pretty black muthfucka. Stink was polished but still rugged. With that aura of improbable existence, he was the only cat Zest knew besides his cousin that made his bones on the streets without drugs being the main source of income. He tagged cars, and ran his operation not only with an iron fist, but like it was a Fortune 500 company.

Stink said, "After that, I'm going down to Miami with my boys, get away for a minute, so if you need me, let me know now, scoob."

The wheels in Zest's brain started rolling. He knew once they caught up with Action, before the smoke cleared, Harlem would be infrared hot, and in order to maintain his lifestyle and elevate it to that of opulence, he needed to make some new connects. "You got peoples out there?"

"Wouldn't call them people, but I do have a constituent in the Pork & Beans. A couple homies in Carol City," Stink told Zest.

"We need some pies, and a whole lot of 'em," Zest replied, that bald head glistening more than the big diamond rings on his pinkies.

Zest peeking at his watch again said, "You got ten minutes."

Zest replied, "That means the boardroom must be close?"

It was. A garage on Washington Height. But the next thing

that came out of Zest mouth made Stink call and tell them he'd be late. Zest had made him an offer he couldn't refuse after hearing about a line for $10,000 apiece. But 100 was the minimum. After some negotiating, all three men agreed to meet in the middle.

For Stink it would be the easiest and most lucrative investment he'd ever made.

Capri was looking for security, answering the "what if's" in advance, concluding that if his retaliatory actions landed him in prison, Christine would make sure his bricks got moved and his bread made it to him.

For Zest it meant the next level! Ever since hearing the anecdotes of Rich Porter and his Mob Style cohorts, he'd dreamed of one day becoming a gangsta don of that caliber but on some new and improved shit. Princess would then have no choice but to forget the stories of the 80s and leave them behind along with everything else when it was all said and done. And he couldn't wait!

Listen I need another whip, this Hummer got me hot, I know it," Capri shot at Stink as Zest looked on.

Stink replied, "You seen the new 850s?"

"Nah, but—"

"I got one for you. Black leather, black paint, black BBSs. Consider it a gift to the father to be."

The more Zest heard Stink speak, the more he was growing on him. But if he came through with those bricks, chances of him doing any wrong in Zest's eyes would be slim to none.

Stink rose to his feet saying, "We all deserve the good life. And just like all who oppose us will get everything they got coming to them, we'll get everything we got coming to us. Just gotta be careful because them alphabet cats come in all shapes, sizes, colors and creeds. They looking like us now. Nothing is sacred anymore."

As they were leaving the restaurant for their cars, Stink had a travel agent friend of his make arrangements for them at the

Green & Blue Diamond Hotel overlooking one of Miami's livest beaches. After hanging up he informed them of the details, and told Capri where to pick the 850 up from, then jumped in his cherry Lex convert' and peeled off blasting Ain't No Nigga. He may've had no priors, but he was as flamboyant as they come.

The Hayward cousins addressed a few more thoughts and concerns as Capri stared his Hummer down dreading the idea of getting back in it. When he looked again he noticed a chick in a tiny skirt and stilettos, her thick nipples penetrating the thin fabric covering very little of her lithe but curvy frame. Her lips had this sheer shimmering champagne gloss, and her eyes were all over Capri like he'd missed a child support payment or some shit.

"Who that?" Zest queried, eyes squinted.

"Bitch name Daffany."

"Not cute as Christine, but so sexy, " Zest grinned as the watched her strut across the street like it belonged to her.

As soon as she was close enough, Capri said, "What are you doing here?"

"My girlfriend called me and said she was riding down Amsterdam and she saw the Hummer, so I got dressed and jumped in a cab because I wanted to see you again after that work you put in the last time we were together." She shifted her bright eyes to Zest, purred, "I got a friend who like short, stock nigga with baldies and goatees, who keep a lot of ice in their ears, on pinkies, and in the charm."

Zest and Capri looked at each other before Zest said, "I'm about to get married, shortie" and stalked towards his Benz.

Capri couldn't help but to release this utter of a chuckle as he dug in his pocket and handed Daffany a few bills. "What's this?" she murmured, hands on her shapely hips.

"Money for you to jump back in a cab."

"Why? I thought—"

"I sent my wife home a few hours ago, and I didn't have to

27

tell her why, so I definitely ain't gotta tell you why," he said trudging towards his big black gas guzzler.

Daffany said, "You ever woke up with your dick in a bitch mouth?"

Hating to admit it, Capri slowed up and looked back, said, "Nah—not yet."

TWO

Daffany was running around straightening up her tiny and desolate apartment when she heard the loud buzzing of her intercom. It was a little after 10 P.M. and she just finished feeding her five year old boy, and daughter of three some canned pasta. It was always her practice to wait until the last minute to get things done, though she'd never admit it. As she looked around she knew she was on hard times, and that if she was to turn it around, and fast, this was her best chance. She wasn't always a scheming stunt, and once upon a time happened to be the prettiest girl on University Avenue. Then she got introduced to thugs and sex, and her dreams of graduating from Spellman were replaced by two kids and 23 years of regrets.

"Who is it?" she shouted into the intercom, and back came, "Pri!"

She buzzed him in then rushed her kids into their room. She knew she frequented too many men to involve her children in her fly-by-night engagements, so she tried hard to conceal her sins. "Come on, my company's on his way up!"

"Mommy, can we take the TV with us? Ain't no lights in there," the little boy complained.

"I don't care, matter fact, I'll bring it to you."

The little girl began to cry, "I want my daddy."

"Shut up! I hope he come het ya lil' fresh ass when he get out! Humph! Now get in that room!" she snapped as she pushed the baby by her head into the room. "Dom, go get the TV and you better not drop it, or be pushing my remote control buttons all hard. And get ya whining ass sister a bottle!"

"She too big for bottles."

"What I said?! I'm the mommy around here!"

Her son followed orders, fully aware that anytime that television made it to the kid's room she had some cat coming through. There were times she didn't let him channel surf so instead he watched her ferociously bob her head between some stranger's legs, though he had no idea what she was doing.

By the time Capri rang the bell, she had her daughter pacified with a bottle of soda and her son preoccupied with his young addiction to television. She quickly splashed a bit of that Gucci Rush on, smeared her lips in cherry gloss, let her braids down, took her robe off, then proceeded to the door. Capri was leaning against the groove of her doorway when she appeared in a tight wife beater and heels. Immediately he peeped the Vivica Fox lookalike wasn't wearing anything below the waist and that thing was waxed Brazilian style.

"What took you so long?" she asked him then spun around, then widespread ass checks dangling as she exploited that A-wide gap separating her long legs leading the way into the dimmed flat.

Capri ran his hand through his short crop of curls as he shut the door behind him, thinking of how long of a day it had been. After going out to Queens to pick up the BMW, he stopped by Christine's and rubbed on her still flat stomach for a while, before playing the block with his little homies, and eventually realizing the only way he'd get the incomparable Action out his thinker was to shoot up to the Bronx to release on a whore.

"Business," he told her, hitting the light switch so he could see what was going on up in there. The light was coming from a crystal chandelier. Beneath it was a large glass table with fingerprints, stains, and an empty fruit basket right beside a brand new coreless phone. Not far from there was a clear view of an empty living room, dull wood floor, a cheap fan sitting in one window and some white shades covering the rest.

"You wasn't playin' when you said you jus' moved in here, huh?"

"Why you say that, cause my house look empty?"

"Yeah. Where the kids at?" he asked as he examined the filthy tabletop.

"I got my furniture on lay-a-way, and I put my kids to sleep."

"Where they at?" he questioned, then pulled his blamer and began to scan the apartment.

"Why you tripping?"

"Bitches be tryna set niggas up! And I'm just makin' sure it just me, you, and ya kids here. Now what room they in?'

She let him see the kids, and gave him a tour of the pad to assure him he was safe. While doing so she, for the first time, realized the game she was playing was a dangerous one.

"You aight now?"

"Be easy! I know how bitches get down. Y'all a set a nigga up with the quickness. And I know too many cats that died up in some pussy, so that's why I skeptical about comin' to see chicks I don't really know. But, I'm good now," he expressed as he took his jacket off and removed his other gun from his waist.

Damn! Not only is this nigga a killa and paid, but he's fine too!, she thought to herself as she walked up on him and wrapped herself in his arms. "This feel so good," she radiantly released, with her eyes shut. She was feeling him, and that was never part of the plan.

"I got a few questions for you?"

"What?"

"How long you been livin' here? Where the fuck am I supposed to sit? And how much more do you owe before you can get ya furniture off lay-a-way?"

She backed him into one of her dining-table chairs, and set on his lap. "For now, we can sit right here. I been here for a few

31

months. And…I owe two more thousand. I used my student loan to put a down payment on the set I want. It's black leather."

"So you in school?"

"No, I signed into a community college just to get the loan, so I could furnish my apartment. But, I been thinkin' about takin' some night classes in September. Why, you gon' look out?"

"I look like a trick?" he arrogantly questioned while finger fucking the coochie.

She took a sigh before saying, "Damn, a nigga gotta be a trick to treat a chick right?"

"I ain't got no problem lookin' out, but be easy! Don't expect to be compensated for the sex, cause then I gotta treat you like a hoe!"

She got up and about-faced, then climbed back onto his lap. "I'm not a hoe, I just know how to show a nigga how much I'm feelin' him, when I feel him."

"Is that the case?" Pri chuckled.

"I'm feelin ya whole gangsta! I know yousa general out there, and I know the chicks be chasin'. I just want in. and, I'm a woman that know what it take to satisfy a man."

She concluded her admission of evident admiration by penetrating his ear with her tongue. Pri slid his hands down her sleek waist and palmed her plump cheeks.

"You gon' bless me or do I gotta pound that pussy out first?"

Just as she was about to entertain the trivial inquiry, her telephone began to ring. "Let me get this. You keep that dick rock-hard for me, please. Be right back," she squealed, eyes on the bulge in his jeans.

Just a few feet into the corridor the ringing was subdued by a, "Hello."

"What took you so long to answer the phone?" the caller immediately asked.

"I got company, that's what. Call me later."

"Who?" the caller haggled.

"Who I told you I was feeling."

"The light skin kid with the Hummer?"

"Yeah, now can you call back later?"

"Not before giving me some details!"

Daffany signed. "Okay. I came to the door in my Gucci shoes, no panties and a tight ass beater that stops just below my navel. Fucked his head up."

"What he got on?!"

"Girl, I don't know. But his pockets got the mumps."

"I already know he getting' it, bitch. Now what he had on!"

"A black Diesel jean suit, a red Diesel beater, red Yankee cap, and some new construction Timbs. His high yellow ass look good," she whispered.

"Girl, he gonna kill you when he find out you ain't Daffany."

"By then I'ma have his fine ass wide open. The first time I gave him head, I sucked the nigga bone dry, swallowed and all that. Gave him a few minutes to gather himself, then sucked him off again in the dressing room of a department store. He ain't getting the snake slobbed like that nowhere else."

"How you know?"

"The nigga's eyes rolled to the back of his head. I can't explain it, it's weird, a good weird. Oh I know, it's like a young nigga experiencing dick sucks for the first time. Tomorrow morning he gonna wake up with his dick in my mouth, and it's gonna be all she wrote."

"Asia, you better be careful because you playing with fire. He ain't those little boys you be milking for they little out of town money. And I think he was locked up for some crazy shit when we was pen pals. I should've never told you I knew him that day at the Boston Ballroom."

"You just pointed me his direction. I been hearing his name in the streets for years, and my daughter's father always screaming the nigga's name like he's God or something. So this was destine to be."

"Girl, you lost your mind this time."

"No I didn't, I found my mind," she shot back then dropped the cordless back on the cradle.

"Who was that, Daffany?" Capri quizzed as he lifted that beater up and over her head.

"My kids godmother being nosy."

"Sounds like the bitch was being nosy, and you were forthcoming."

After seeing and feeling her nakedness, he wasn't even concerned with what she'd said or had to say. Her breasts were round, full, ripe and soft—centered by perky brown nipples and honey colored halos. He leaned in and began sucking the right one rather greedily, her ass in his palms. By the time he got the left breast, his hands corralling both C-cups, she was loving his consumption, the manhandling, his unapologetic demeanor. Moans she hadn't heard in years escaped her, exciting him even more.

"Hold up, let me turn some music on," she whispered then walked over to ta portable disc player. Capri watched and couldn't help but agree with Zest. She wasn't all that cute, but she was five-feet-eight-inches of sexiness. "this my shit right here, Pri. Always wanted to fuck to this."

"Fuck?"

"Yeah, my days of just getting fucked been over."

Do Me Baby, by Mellisa Morgan filled the dining area. It wasn't loud, but there was enough volume to camouflage what was to come. For a moment they just appraised each other. She, his muscles. Her, her curves. It was the prettiness of her nipples that brought Capri back to her breasts. But she had other ideas. With her lush body, breasts against his chest, she backed him into a stumble that had him leaned back against a wall with a smirk. She then fell to her knees and unfastened his belt. He watched intently as she pulled his erection from his jeans, and held it firmly, tonguing the slit. Then she spat on it. Licking her lips, she leered up to hear him say, "Fuck was that about?"

"Lubricant. The wetter and sloppier, the better, baby pop," she chimed, this salacious glare on her face that remained as she took as much of his length as she could in her mouth.

Capri relaxed, his hand atop her head, and she went to work maneuvering her mouth. The cheery lip gloss, saliva and tongue ring brought about immediate pleasure. The sound affects—priceless. "Wait. Can't see your face," Capri sneered, on the verge of ecstasy.

Accommodating Capri, she pushed her micro braids over her shoulder, crawled a little closer and reacquainted her lips with his penis, missing no spot, making no mistakes. Peering sown on her, Capri grabbed her head with both hands this time, hissing, "Shit!" Wielding her power over him, her focus shifted from the shaft to the head to an effortless deep throat, and Capri could no longer withstand. That heat from deep within made his legs weaken, breathing thicken, his eyes roll to the back of his head. She felt him tense up, the throb, and pulled the hard flesh from her mouth as a heavy load of semen shot out spewing all over her lips, chin, neck, and welcoming tits.

"Mmmm," she simpered taking a sexy stance. "That was a heavy load of spunk there! Now have a seat boo, so I can skeet too." Before he was seated she had him to full length again, meat packaged in ultra-sensitive latex he provided. Slowly, she climbed on, her eyes on his, and turned out to be tighter than expected. At first she winched, but her powerfully rotating hips swayed generating genius gyration, and within moments that moist cleft lessened and became water park wet. Bottom lip between her teeth, halfway to euphoria, she rocked back and forth, up and down, side to side, round and round.

"Shit!" she grunted, the physical sensation meeting that of the mental.. she could feel that rush about to burst and locked on to his shoulders while bouncing that thing.

"Goddamn," Capri cursed, bucking back, her hips in his

grasps, the chair on the verge of tilting. The flow felt so good, had it not been for the semen spangling from her face, he'da been kissing the shit out of her.

Sensing how enthralled Capri was, and on the cusp of that climax, she got wilder—to the point that he slipped out of her as she nearly fell panting and laughing. She'd got one off, but when she checked, the rubber was empty. That excited her even more. "Getup," she urged, his hand in hers. As he stood to his towering six feet, she said, "You seem like you're somewhere else, too reserved. Loosen up." She then bent over and touched her toes, adding, "I wasn't you to go so deep, I feel you in my soul."

That why he was there.

To release. For escape. From mental anguish. From reality. So he parked behind her, grabbed a hold of her round hips, held on like they were reins, and plowed his way into the slight slit between her legs, and quickly caught speed.

"Yeah, just like that, Capri," she moaned looking back over her shoulder. "But harder, nigga. Harder! Harder! Mmhmm, just like that! Do me baby…like I've never been done before."

Capri was like a bulldozer, pounding away, and she was quickly losing her footing. Couldn't feel him in her soul, but she could feel him in the pit of her stomach, his breath on her back. And then her heel turned over, spoiling the flow. Quickly she reclaimed her stance to find that the condom was still empty. She pulled it off and took him all the way down her throat, sucking hard and to perfection.

"I'm about to bust," he stammered while holding the back of her head and fucking her mouth. "You the truth, the best I ever had."

This times he swallowed, taking it all in while envisioning the bigger picture. Becoming his high paid mistress. It wasn't the loftiest of goals, but life was no longer about love for this one. it was about security and survival. "You cool up there?" she quizzed still squatting before his now flaccid dick.

"It was everything a nigga expected. That straight make-a-nigga-bust head," he replied staring her down. He was so gone she went from resembling Vivica to rivaling the thespian.

"Thank you," she gushed feeling accomplished. Everything was going as she'd planned, until his phone started chirping. She ambled towards the adjacent kitchen for a rag and Palmolive, and he went for his jacket. She could help but release that angst filled sigh, mad at herself for failing to turn his phone off.

Just outside the kitchen, "I see you took my orders lightly," had invaded Capri's thought. That sinister voice was unmistakable.

"Action!"

"You were supposed to call me right after the youngsta gave you my message. I watched you and him politick, watched you encourage him to defy me. When I shut a block down and niggas come back out—you know what happens next right? Black sedans, black suits, flowers, and songs dedicated to homies."

"how you got my number?"

Ignoring Capri's query, Action said, "I was watching from afar when you pulled up in your back Humvee. I saw you entertaining you little following. Son, don't get them kids killed. I'm telling you, you don't wanna see me angry. Especially when all you had to do was call me when my daughter delivered the first message."

"How you get my number?!"

"Caller ID at Mecca's spot," Action remarked slyly, oblivious to Mecca's revelations, to Pearl Hayward's corroboration.

"Stay the fuck away from them!"

"Or what?"

Capri took the phone from his ear and glared at it. "we need to rap. Meet me in Central Park by the Onasis Reservoir. Neutral ground," Capri stated remembering Zest's mentioning of a clear view of the reservoir from his Central Park West apartment.

Action laughed. "neutral ground? What you think we going through something? Because if that's what you're thinking you're just as foolish as I had you being. And for the record I don't go through shit, I wipe niggas out before it even gets that far."

This nigga talking that talk, Capri thought, the sprawling reality and severity of the situation bringing him to his feet. "I don't wanna see you, you wanna see me. Onasis Reservoir."

"Hey, young nigga, I'm callin' the shot around here! Midnight Express Diner, one hour!" the line went dead.

Capri shoved his phone in his pocket, tossed his jacket on, shouted, "Yo Daffany, I'm out. I gotta bounce."

Soapy rag in hand, soapy breast, she appeared vexed and saying, "You told me you were spending the night. And my name's not Daffany, it's Asia. Daffany's my girlfriend."

With the music playing, Action's audacious undertone resonating loudly, and Christine's safety being of paramount importance—Capri didn't register shit she was saying.

"Listen, here's a grand, go get your furniture, Daffany."

And just like that he was gone.

THREE

Zest and Nickels were seated behind the tinted windows of the Expedition when the shifts changed at the Bronx County Supreme Courthouse. The light drizzle bounced off the windshield as they got blunted, patiently awaiting their next victim to appear.

"Zest, why you think we catch bodies and destroy families? Shit like that always be on my mind bee. And I can't escape the thought."

Zest was numb to murder, had been since that fateful day back in Yonkers the first time he touched a gun. Things had never been the same since, for him or his first murder victim. "I don't know. It's all part of the game. And sometimes the wrong people catch the short end of the stick," Zest replied, screwing the silencer onto his Smith & Wesson revolver.

"Ever think about what it would be like to catch the short end of that stick?"

Zest looked over at his main man, and with conviction, replied, "Nah, I'm great at what I do. And for that to happen, a nigga gotta catch me sleepin', and I never sleep."

"I think about it," Nickels returned, smoke slowly streaming from his nostrils. "I be wondering how I'll be remembered. Who'd attend my funeral. Who'd look after my seeds. What the afterlife might be like. I wonder if the nigga that body me'll have the balls to come to my wake like we've done in the past. I know I'd go straight to hell for all the niggas I melted. Nut I wouldn't bitch up, I'd still rep hard!"

"Fuck having thoughts about dying. I'm too busy try'na find new places to stash all the money. I'm running out of stash spots, kid!" Zest laughed.

Nickels took a pull off the blunt, then said, "Yo, I been hustling since I was thirteen, ten-fuckin'-years, and I'm only holding a little over forty thou'. I can't keep paper. See, you rarely spend, then you ain't got no kids, so I know you caked up."

Zest focused on the approaching pedestrians, as he told Nickels, "I ain't nowhere close to where I'm headed. And neither are you."

"Bee, I got four kids, three baby mothers, two that live with me with my two daughter, a lil' brother—and I'm looking out for every last one of them. Imagine if my moms would take my offers, I'd be what they call hustling backwards,"

Parked adjacent to the whip Shyann carpooled in, they pulled their hats below their brows, when Zest said, "That's the bitch right there. She coming our way right...now."

"With the nigga with the stupid walk?"

"Yeah, they right there."

"Fuck that clown doing with that bad bitch?"

"I have no idea. But he's in the wrong place at the wrong time, and they're about to get plucked together. Another short-end-of-the-stick nigga."

The second the couple neared their ride, the doors on the Expo swung open and both men hoped out swinging iron. "Shyann, come here. Let me holla at you!"

Shyann squinted trying to see through the mist. "Who that? I can't see your face."

"It's me," Zest stated casually, tapping the trigger of his .44 pistol. The first slug to exit the instrument of destruction snagged her torso, ripping right through her and forcing her backwards.

"Muthafuck...!" she sputtered a millisecond before the

40

second slug cracked her face, causing her frame to collapse.

Roger watched in horror as his colleague and lover died instantly. He was to propose that night. But instead he was wiping rain from his eyes as though what he'd witnessed was somehow a mirage. But he quickly realized it was all real when he saw Zest raise the ratchet to his face and squeeze off. Roger took an exit wound that sent his thinker flying out the back of his skull.

Nickels was impressed by Zest's sharp shooting, but quickly urged they get ghost and place some distance between them and the carnage. From behind the steering wheel, ripping through the rain slicked streets, he said, "Where to now?"

"Slow up. Fish and chips spot on One-twenty-seventh and Eighth Avenue. I want something to eat. Then take me to get my coupe," Zest instructed, dialing Capri's number.

Capri had just sped passed the courthouse when his phone began to sound off. He was floating through a string of green lights with the mini-Mac in his lap, a blunt of Hydro between his lips, and murder on his mind. He didn't answer his phone until he ran a red light. "Yo!"

"Pri, what up? Why you ain't answer ya horn?"

"I'm behind the wheel."

"What up, you aiight? You sound like you tight about something. Where you at?"

"On my way to Midtown to see the old man."

"You wasn't gonna tell me?" Zest snapped.

"Where you at?"

"One-fifty-first and Eighth."

"Listen, meet me at the Midnight Express Diner."

"What up with dude?"

"His days is getting shorter as my heart grow colder, that's all I'ma say, peoples."

"I feel you. Bust it, that other thing. Done!"

"Good. Wish I could've been there to see that rotten-ass bitch squirm. I'll see you in a few," Capri said hanging up, then sought the fastest route to midtown realizing he only had twenty minutes left.

FOUR

I t was almost midnight, and got the last couple hours
Action's latest chum sat amongst the ranks watching cats
of his vocation pass off significant portions of money.
Some was offerings, some was owned, bust most of it was
extorted. One kid had actually paid a ransom note. Action
would flick through the hefty mitts, sniff the neatly wrapped
stacks and bundled bills while pretending he really had concern
for the spineless twerps. His notorious reputation alone
discouraged cats, disheartened crews, some of the strongest
niggas in the streets. And what was scary was he didn't have
picks, no favorites, just targets. At 50 and already wealthy, not a
day went by without him position himself for the windfall. And
he never collected in the same place twice. Kept the police and
conspiracies attempting to eradicate him at a minimum.

Slouched back in a significantly large booth located in the
rear of the diner, Action as always, was the center of attraction.
Donned in navy blue denim and some boots from Italy, he
feasted on buffalo wings and onion rings, fraternizing with his
manz, and feeling out the cat to his left seeking his assistance.
Brother Joe, a certified killer, and ordained minister, a
credential obtained through the mail from Modesto, California,
had been around just as long as Action, which is why he served
as underboss. Destro, a bucktooth, little scrawny pervert in his
mid 40s, was Action's longtime friend and the third in
command. Both were present. And so was Mumbles and

Tragedy, two other high ranking members of Action's faculty responsible for their share of havoc – several unsolved murders, a few kidnappings, and a whole lot of other shit.

"You gon' eat with me or what, Richie Rich?" Action asked facetiously. "If we gonna be breaking bread together, might as well start now."

"I'm cool," the youngster stated, his fingertips drumming the table.

"My man Capri should be here real soon, " said Action as he glanced at his platinum watch. "Have patience, it'll take you far in the streets. And eat. Best onion rings on the island of Manhattan."

Swallowing the smallest morsel would've made the kid sicker than he already was. He had no idea how this would go, what exactly to expect from Capri or Action when his proposal was presented. And "Midnight Express Diner, one hour!" kept echoing in his head knowing Capri would be coming through that front door any minute.

"So what makes you thing Zest had something to do with the home invasion that left your moms and brother dead?" Tragedy asked.

"For about a month now I been hearing that this dame name Princess is the number one supplier of Ecstasy, and that she's his woman," the kid replied while thinking of how much Tragedy resembled a pitbull with a full beard and a missing tooth.

Action looked up, but continued stuffing his face and pockets, as niggas filed in and out of the diner setting it out. There was so much movement that folks running the diner had no idea what was going on, and didn't seem to care so long as money was being made.

"Things are tight right now with Maribelle just giving birth a few days ago. But it's all big bills there this time, like you wanted," muttered some slim, brown skin pretty boy in a Pelle leather and A-Solo boots as he slipped the old man a stuffed envelope.

"You think I give a fuck about you domestic bullshit? Every time I turn around that broad's pregnant. When Tackhead put his man Lava on yo ass, trying to move you off the block, I didn't come to you, you came to me," Action spat, licking ranch dressing from his fingers.

"And you vouched for me. But I didn't think I'd be parting ways with 10K every month."

Action looked at the nigga like he was crazy. "What's this anyway?"

"Seven thousand."

"So you short three," Action shot back as he stuck another wing in his mouth. "Know what that means, right?"

The kid looked at Action's counterparts, then the familiar face amongst them before saying, "No, I don't. I never been late or short."

"Tell 'em, Mumbles," Action ordered.

"You walk back to the Bronx," Mumbles mumbled bringing about a little laughter.

The kid looking to recover a half million in Ecstasy pills, and permission to hit Zest began to question himself. Whether or not he'd made the right decision bringing his grievance to Action. He'd heard the stories. The unyielding association cats got themselves in for seeking his aid. How he became that silent partner you only saw once a month. The price paid for underworld ties. All he wanted was retribution without being extorted, and losing his dignity like the kid he was eyeing in the mean Pelle. "What?'

He quipped in disbelief.

Action said, "The easy way or the hard way."

The kid thought of a disgruntled comrade who'd gone missing about a year ago. Straight disappeared. Reluctantly, he handed the keys to his Porsche over, then stormed out the door in a frenzy right pass Nickels and Zest. They stalked in and looked around to notice they'd beat their unsung capo to

Action's feeding ground. Without being detected, they slid into a booth by the door, each on one side of the table, and placed their orders.

"I see Action and 'em, but ain't no sign of old boy."

"He should be here any minute," Zest assured Nickels.

"You never did tell me why old boy wanted girlie gone," Nickels poked.

"She was threatening to lay a track on a home invasion we did a few months ago," Zest whispered, half his body over the tabletop, his face just inches from Nickels. "I don't think she'da went through with the threat, but can't take that chance. Too much at stake. Just got a new connect, I'm about to propose, and we shooting down to Miami in a couple days. Had to be done."

"Who you going to Miami whit?" Nickels quizzed.

"Me, Pri and Stink."

While Zest was giving him the bare minimum of details, their orders arrived. But before they could dig into the fish sandwiches and apple pie, Capri slid in with his baseball cap crazy low. He had both hands in his jacket pockets as he proceeded straight to Action's gathering.

"Why so many men if we ain't warring?" Capri asked as looked all Action's cohorts in the face, his eyes resting on the unfamiliar one.

"Capri, I called you here to discuss business. Now have a seat," Action urged while motioning for Mumbles and Tragedy to get up so Capri could slide in.

"If I don't have a seat, what?" Capri snapped.

Zest and Nickels peeped Capri's demeanor and wasted no time joining the party. Destro, Tragedy, and Brother Joe noticed them vastly approaching and leveled the menus that held their guns beneath. Action was outraged by what he deemed disrespect.

"Fall back," Action ordered his men. "Capri, tell them little niggas to beat it."

Neither of the men were really ready to die, or to find out what life after death was really like, but no one budged. The patrons and employees looked on oblivious to the potential danger, figuring it was just another of those Hip Hop spats entourages go through. "Need I repeat myself?" Action sneered, buying time to slip back into his bulletproof Pea Coat and kufi just in case the slugs did fly.

Action's crew backed off, Zest and Nickels released a little of the tension in their postures, and Action slid out from the booth moving towards Capri. He grabbed Capri's arm like he was a child and headed towards the rest area. Of course Capri resisted, yanking his arm free, even stared Action down, making Richie Rich all more weary.

"What is your problem?" Action seethed into Capri's ear.

"What's understood needs no explanation."

"Excuse me?" asked Action.

"You heard what I said."

That made Action furious. "All eyes are on us. The phone area. Now."

Adrenaline flowing at top speed, Capri took a gander in that direction, see if he could possible hit Action back there then slide off into the night. The phones happened to be in the same region of the diner as the rest rooms. And there was a lot of traffic back there. But he still went. As soon as they were in what little seclusion available, Action said, "That shit you just pulled could've gotten people killed. I told you to come alone. And you bring that dope fiend and Zest like I'ma have your shell hit or something."

"Sorry to disappoint you, but it is what it is."

"And what is that?"

"I don't trust you."

"what is this world coming to?" Action laughed. "There's no mystery I'm not to be trusted. But I'm beginning to wonder about you."

"You shut the block down, barge up in my chick's crib, you

should be wondering."

Action cut his eyes at Capri, said, "You didn't show up to my 50ᵗʰ birthday bash. Didn't respond to the message I sent through Katrina. So that was the only way I could get your attention. And on top of that, no one, I mean no one disrespects my daughter."

"Your daughter, huh?" Capri snarled, shaking his head.

Action began to wonder if Capri knew about the '77 fling with Mecca that produced Christine. Nah, he reasoned, his arms folded across his massive chest. "I thought I taught you to respect gangstas?"

"You did, but that was before I became a Street General."

"Those little specs of success you're enjoying can quickly be erased. When did you become so defiant?"

"Coming up without a mother and father made me this way," Capri stated in a tone that made Action's face foil. "Now what do you want from me?"

"You think I don't know you killed Lux and took Brother Joe's smack out the apartment? Think I don't know y'all ripped off a half mil' in E-pills yous didn't report on that sting I put you on a few months ago. I deserve nothing less," Action barked turning the heat up.

"I don't know what you talking about."

"You know I live with a lot of remorse and some of the things I've done, I still don't understand. Maybe it was greed, or lust, or love. Maybe it was betrayal or disloyalty. But with age come wisdom. For me, fifty years of wisdom."

"What is this, a confessional? Some sort of intervention?" Capri replied with a blithe disregard.

Action released a chilling chuckle, and out of it came, "I destroyed a lot of niggas. Young, ungrateful, arrogant niggas just like you. That's what I'm getting at, young nigga."

Capri released the same sardonic laughter Action had just moments ago, then said, "Old man you on my time and you still ain't tell me what you want from me."

Action was tight. His jaw, his stomach, his fists. Clearly this wasn't going the way he thought it would. Capri was too poised, too confident, too calculated. And he wasn't used to seeing that. But if the dead weight ploy worked, leaving Lux a casualty, surely Action would have to try again. "The name Richie Rich ring any bells?"

Capri recalled the first time hearing the name, the home invasion, and how deadly it had turned out. Even thought of Shyann and her recent demise. "What's this about?"

"He wants revenge for the senseless murders of his momma and kid brother."

"Why the fuck are you telling me?"

"Because Zest and Princess' names are in the mix real heavy. And I thought you should know."

"And how do you know this?"

"He's out there at the table," Action finagled in there like he was talking about those onion rings. And before Capri could ask the question, Action said, "No, he doesn't know Zest is here."

"You can't be serious???"

"It's called business, and I'm in the business of lining my pockets. So when opportunity falls in my lap, I react."

"But you set the whole thing up, why would he come to you?"

"He doesn't know that," Action snickered. "And all he wants is retribution without war. This kid is loaded. We could spin this our way. That's why we're here. We're supposed to be negotiating a surrender."

"And who's surrendering?" Capri wanted to know, his hands back in his jacket pockets, clutching the two concealed revolvers.

"His mother's killer."

The traits of a snake were never missing from Action, but that night his fangs were on full display. And with all he now knew, it was cleat to Capri that Action was a king cobra. The snake of all snakes, slithering freely through his shadowy

49

underworld. Capri's right hand moved to his mouth, heartbeat thumping, armpits dampening. This was surreal. Shit that does down in the hood. But not to him. Not to his. He wasn't even 23 yet, and it felt like he was going through a mid-life crisis, and very close to meeting his threshold. The anger within made his eyes water, but there was no way he was giving Action the honor of seeing a tear tumble. But it wouldn't be long before his brand of justice would be meted out.

Capri said, "I'd like a little revenge too, but we don't always get what we want - do we?"

Action was left standing alone and stuck, his conscience chumping at him. But his mind quickly shifted to the next plan of action: taking Richie Rich for bad now, instead of bleeding him for years to come.

He had Mumbles pay their tab as they headed for the door. Richie Rich was wondering why they were leaving and Capri and his crew were still seated. While he wondered, just loud enough so that Brother Joe, Destro and Zac could hear him, Action decided, "First thing, I never ever wanna see them three together again. State with the Rican, then the pussy whipped nigga. Capri, I'll deal with myself. Trunk Rich now, take him to the spot, and it's all or nothing."

That caught all the men by surprise.

Destroy said, "As in?"

"If he doesn't tell us where the stash is, kill him. If he does, kill him."

Zac, a trigger happy fool, and sometimes overzealous when it comes to following orders said, "I'll handle Nickels, and leave Zest to Mumbles."

Just as Mumbles joined them, Action nodded and Brother Joe grabbed Rich who saw it coming, jamming his gun in his ribcage. Simultaneously, shots rang out. Rapid fire. As if practiced, Action hit the deck, Zac blanketed, and Destro and Brother Joe returned fire.

Capri and his crew watched from the diner, ready to attack.

But they were now the focal point of those who weren't running for cover, so all they could do was observe. That's when Zest noticed the cat behind the trigger was the pretty boy in the Pelle that had walked by them when they arrived. He'd reached his breaking point.

"Oooh, shit!"

FIVE

Adjusting to life back in the northeastern section of the country wasn't east for Trent, having spent significant portions of the last two years in Virginia training young agents how to conduct themselves in the line of fire. The house he'd built in Yonkers was always tranquil and filled with pure unabridged joy upon his return – Mary made sure of that. But something was different, and she could tell. He was leaner and more muscular, but that wasn't it. Her 42-year old husband of twenty years seemed nervous and distant. Law enforcement being livelihood as well, she'd worked numerous murder cases, logged countless hours, solved some, and watched murderers walk she knew was guilty. So she knew what it felt like to be mentally elsewhere. As she watched him move about shirtless, sex stoked her imagination and she wanted to feel him between her 44-year old thighs. Since nineteen sexuality had always been a natural part of life to her, and it showed when she walked up behind Trent in their lounge area and grabbed his bare chest.

Trent spun around to see a woman he married at a time when it was taboo for a black man to have a white woman; when the country wasn't far removed from segregation. The 5'4", 135-lb detective, was dressed in black pants and a beige blouse, fit to perfection. With her dark hair, bright eyes, and olive skin tone, she looked better now than she did the day they took their vows. "Hey, you," he said, his hands resting on the small of her back.

And after looking in his green eyes and moving her hands to his lower back, she said, "You seem distracted. I hope this assignment in Harlem isn't personal and only professional."

Trent knew exactly what she was talking about. His only daughter's depraved lover/ "I do my job. It's never personal. He's a grown man, and the decisions he make will determine his successes and his failures."

Mary's grasp lost strength, and Trent noticed it, the ringing of the phone severing the whole embrace. In long strides, Trent moved towards the ringing, picked up and immediately heard, "McCants , please!"

"Atkins?"

"Yeah, it's me. Just got a call from Jackson encouraging us to report to the scene of a double homicide on the Eastside of the Bronx. Bronx County Supreme Courthouse. Cause of death, gunshot wounds. I'm not staying too far from there, so I'm on my way now."

"I'm leaving right now!" Trent said loud enough that Mary heard it as well. She sent an encouraging smile his way, one he'd shot her in the past when duty called, and noted that moment as one that would take their lives for an insipid turn.

"And then we're to make our way to another murder scene in midtown. Was reported less than an hour ago," Agent Atkins added.

"Where?"

"The Midnight Express Diner."

Trent said, "Did you contact the fellas down there?"

"Said it started in the diner and spilled out onto the streets. Two Hip Hop crews, so the eye witnesses say."

"Somehow I know Anwar Outen was involved."

"Yeah?"

"Absolutely. When he sneezes, the streets feel the draft."

"Then why kill, why get his hands dirty, bring this type of heat if he has that much influence?"

Trent holstered his weapon, the fastened himself into his Kevlar vest and said, "The natural evolution of criminals. Their pathetic, petulant asses get more pettier the more power they acquire!"

"You lost me McCants."

"Sustainability. Staying power. If he doesn't maintain his leverage, a young gun will sneak up and take it. Criminal voyeurism of the past – John Gotti taking big Paul out and becoming boss of the Gambino Crime Family."

"And you think he's involved?"

"I'm sure he is, and if it did start in the diner, and the cameras were rolling, there should be some good footage available."

If Trent had it right, this could be the debacle of some of the street's most influential players; exactly what the Manhattan District Attorney and police commissioner had in mind when the decision was made to implant the experienced unit into Harlem. And, Trent's unsuspected rise in rank.

Of course it was personal!

SIX

About 20 miles south, in the borough of Queens, two experienced shooters sat outside of Gordon's strip club on Hillside Avenue. They'd been tailing a target for approximately two hours. From midtown to a garage where he switched cars, through the city and across the Queens Borough Bridge, just waiting for the right time to start their shit, separate his body from his soul, they get ghost.

"What way to go out," Capri mentioned, putting the finishing touches on a blunt he'd dumped a whole fifty of Thai weed in.

"The deed ain't done yet," replied Zest, sunk in the driver's seat.

"Nigga, I'm talking about Richie Rich!"

"The saying is true, bullets ain't got no names on 'em."

"Nah, it's called – you get what your hand call for. Not just the Rich kid, I'm talking about Action. He was supposed to cut the check for the old man in exchange for the surrender of his mother's killer."

"Who killed his mother?"

Capri glanced over at Zest, said, "You."

"You bullsinttin', right?"

"That's what the whole get-with-him shit was about. The home invasion in the Bronx."

Zest shook his head, laughed. "That nigga set the whole shit up!"

55

"Same thing I said." "Well, that nigga dead now, thanks to the extended clip in that Mac and a couple bad shots. Wish he'd hit the old man, then he'd be one less nigga we gotta torch."

Capri thought of Trent and how quick things had already spun out of control. But he was living for him, and no one could feel his pain. He got a job to do but so do I!, Capri reasoned putting flames to that blunt.

Zest said, "You know I got the ring, right?"

"What ring?"

"For Princess."

"Can I ask you a question?"

"What?"

"Why you wanna marry her?"

"She make me keep that pep in my step. Stay sharp on my toes. She treats me like a don, and the sex is the bomb. Gets no better."

"Just watch yourself, because when things are too good to be true, they usually aren't."

"What's that about, Pri?"

"I just think she's too quick to be about you, too fast to entertain whatever you promote."

"Isn't that what every nigga wants?"

"After they've been around they city twice," Capri reasoned. "Nigga, you'll be twenty-three and in the last three years I only recall you popping one other chick. And the only reason you popped that is because she had a hit record out."

"Nah, I knocked her down because you wanted her manager. You thought because she had them dick suckin' lips she was gonna give you face. I couldn't a care less about her being on the radio!"

"She did give me face," Capri remembered. "Now back to this ring thing--+

"I'm doing it,...as soon as we get back from Miami," Zest made clear then reached for his bald head with both hands.

"Let's slide up in there, see what's taking this nigga so long, bee."

"Man, I ain't going in there!"

"Nigga, you mad? Let me find out you mad?"

"For what? We followed to three different strip clubs. Shouldn't be much longer now. I say we wait here."

And that they did while pulling on that thick blunt and listening to an old school Kid Capri blend tape. For a brief moment no words were exchanged. The two just stared out into the dampened street, the effect of marijuana allowing them to enjoy Stephanie Mills' Rush over Eric B and Rakim's Paid In Full instrumental. Then the silence was broken with, "<y nigga about to be a father!"

Capri said, "If you too are so in love, how come she never popped up pregnant?"

"I don't know...maybe she doesn't ovulate. Or maybe because she like it in the ass, and in the mouth," Zest remarked rather sharply. "Or maybe because she likes me to splash on her back, her tits, in her face. Something you know nothing about."

Capri looked over at Zest, said, "If that's what ,makes you happy, I salute you."

"Bullshit!" Zest barked.

"Real talk. She bet' not cross you though."

Moments later Destro emerged from the club like a gentleman, town young nubile strippers under each arm. For the first time that night he wasn't looking over his shoulder the way he normally did. Too busy grinning. On the strippers' faces were traces of victory, and in their eyes were dollar signs. For a man of his stature, his extra curriculum activities were unsound.

In nothing short of a carefree manner Destro fondled the females as they moved briskly towards his all black Eldorado. He hit the alarm, the head lights blinked, then they all climbed into the pretty sedan. Both chicks got cozy up front with him, the one closest taking his fedora from his head and sitting it on hers.

As Zest pulled off behind him, Capri said, "And to think, I

used to respect that cat."

They tailed him to a residential area right off of Springfield Boulevard where he parked then killed the engine. When Zest pulled up beside him, Destro's head was wedged between the supple tits of the brown skinned broad, head so deep he didn't even notice that he was being ambushed.

Zest jumped out, snatched the driver's side door open , and dragged Destro's frail frame from the Caddy like he was a rag doll. For the first time in his long career Destro was defenseless. No help to him, his gun was beneath the driver seat.

With the brim of his cap sitting just above his eyelids, Capri hopped out with his semi-auto exposed and approached the passenger side door, yanking it open just as the female reached for the power lock. He said, "Ayyo, y'all break out. Go 'head, bounce! Leave! Now."

"Come one, Shelly! Run, they got guns! These niggas is bugging, boo!" the light skin dame stammered, her doe eyes on Capri trying to see if she recognized him from the club.

That didn't go over too smoothly with Capri, thus he shot the bitch in the abdomen. Just once. Made her fold over in agony, clutching her stomach as she released a horrifying squeal. He then told the one with her breasts exposed, Destro's hat atop her head, "Sorry about your friend. If you don't wanna end up like her, break the fuck out, 'fore I squeeze off on you too!"

She took a gander at her buddy, peeped the preponderance of blood ruining the outfit she'd just loaned her then ran off into the night never once looking at Capri, her tits still out.

From his spot on the curb, Destro said, "It is what it is, so let's have it. I watched you niggas come up, I know what it's hitting for."

"Oh yeah?" Capri quizzed in a sarcastic slur, blunt hanging from his mouth. "Sext, put that nigga in the can."

"I ain't getting in no fucking van. You niggas gon' do y'all right here. Fuck I look like?" Destro declared as his eyes moved to the wounded stripper trying to crawl from the Caddy.

Capri shut the door on her as he watched Zest grip Destro by the collar and snatch him to his feet, pistol to his dome. The stripper's eyes fell shut and her head back right before they pulled off with Destro.

"what's this about?" Destro pled as he watched his car through the back window getting smaller and smaller. "That shit at the restaurant?" if it is, we can smooth that out."

Capri glared at the rearview, said, "It's called redemption. So, repent you sins."

"The hell are you talking about?"

This area of Queens consisted of very few traffic lights, and several STOP signs. As soon as Capri hit a Stop sign, he turned around and slapped the shit of Destro.

"Hey man!" Destro howled.

Two in the morning Capri's phone rang. He knew it could be no one but, "Christine?"

"Yeah, it's me. My mom has a logbook she wants you to see."

"I'm busy right now, but you're gonna be my eyes. Now read to me what you see in the logbook pertaining to Olivia Hayward."

All the air was let out of Destro when he heard that. And it made the onslaught that much easier to deliver when Capri heard, "Date, November, 21 1987. Name, Olivia Hayward. Conditions, dead on arrival. Pri, you hear me?"

Eyes welling up, Capri said, "Yeah, go ahead."

"Two gunshot wounds to the back of the skull, one through the spleen."

"And what are you reading from>" asked Capri headed for the Van Wick Expressway.

"A logbook from the Harlem Hospital, the month of November 1987."

"Thank you, baby."

"Welcome. Where are you?"

"Miami. How you feeling? Is the baby kicking yet?"

"Oh..." she signed as she sadly plopped down on the sofa and placed the logbook on her lap. "Miami, huh?"

"Yeah, on some b.i.," he replied, sensing her discomfort. "Won't be long though. Is the baby moving yet?"

"No, I'm not even showing yet, Capri," Christine answered warmly, finding the inquiry to be very compassionate. "I miss you."

"Miss you too. I'll be calling though," he told her, then said, "Put Mecca on the phone."

In seconds Mecca said, "Hey."

"just wanted to thank you for moving out like that."

"Just do me a favor," she returned.

"And what is that?"

"Be careful, please. Christine told me. And they're gonna need you around here."

Before Capri could respond Christine was back, saying, "She's really happy about being a grandmother."

"What about you, how you feel about it?"

"It wasn't planned, and I did want to go to college, but I have no regrets. What about you, how do you feel?"

"Like, after nine years, I'll finally have someone again who's gonna love me no matter what, that I'll love no matter what, like my moms loved me, like I loved her."

"You'll have both of us," Christine whispered in this sultry undertone.

"Thanks. Call me tomorrow."

She blew him a kiss then hung up.

As Capri tried gathering himself, his thoughts, Destro said, "So you done went and seeded up the big man's daughter, huh?"

"Shut up!" barked Capri.

"And Mecca's fine ass been running her mouth," Destro continued. "Told Action when we found out you was laying your head there, them two bitches were up to no good. Ain't nothing like a woman scorned; I tell you no lies."

"Listen bee, you got two choices - die slow or die fast?" Capri offered periodically glancing back over his shoulder.

"Which one is it gonna be?" Zest asked, nudging Destro with his .44 revolver.

As he eyed down the young goons about to play judge and jury, an unspeakable reverie seized Destro. It was late November, 1987. A cold night in Harlem, winds whistling in the projects, and money being made faster than they could count it. He'd just hit two lines of raw heroin, a half gram in each nostril, and was higher than the clouds when he walked into the building, housing their headquarters, to find his ace-boon and Olivia, just two feet separating them. As always he was secretly turned on by the high yellow beauty's cocky bowlegged stance. She was dressed to the hilt, and Action was in fatigues and Timbs. Everything seemed cool, then he noticed black .32 in Action's right hand, and a .22 Dillinger in Olivia's. Destro was stuck in a haze until he saw Olivia raise her pistol and Action squeeze off in self-defense hitting her in the pelvic region. Her 125-lb body collapsed on impact, blood turning the front of her white fox coat red. Because of the small proximity of the building lobby, the single shot sounded like and M-80 had gone off. In a quick effort to further prove his loyalty, Destro insisted the man-eating fatale be killed for her defiance, and that he be given the honor of going the deed. Action loved Olivia too much though, and quickly ruled against it. Olivia listened as they wrangle about her life, but she wasn't leaving her only child behind without a fight. She was experiencing excruciating pain, but still managed to send shots their way from her crouching position against a wall of mail boxes. She popped her heat at both men grazing Destro, missing Action's blowout by inches, and sealing her own fate.

Back in the present, and in his most defiant of tones, Destro said, "I don't cop pleas, I don't take deals, and I told Action we should've been put both you niggas in the fucking ground years ago! No look – "

Before Destro could complete that sentence, further insult their gangsta, Zest fixed his revolver on Destro's temple and splattered his final thoughts all over the back seat and rear window right there on the Express Way.

SEVEN

BORNX, NEW YORK
235 A.M.

"McCants," Trent announced upon his arrival at the courthouse murders. The whole area was taped off, crime scene investigators scanning for evidence while other policemen stood post. "I'm with a special crime's intelligence unit operating out of the 32nd precinct. And this is my partner, Agent Craig Atkins."

"Okay?" said a thick mustached lieutenant Anglo descent, his skin as pale as the white hat and shirt he wore. He lifted his cigar from his mouth, then grilled the two men of color standing before him. "Talk! I got two fucking bodies, and no witnesses. What do you want?"

Agent Atkins, a stout cat with red freckles and cropped hair, said "We got a call informing us one of the bodies in those bags is a Harlem resident, Shyann Jenkins, and that information here could be viable to our investigation."

"Talk to the fucking sergeant in charge," the lieutenant replied then placed his cigar back in his mouth giving off his aura of importance.

Trent walked off appalled by the lieutenant's lack of camaraderie, lack of respect, his absence of professionalism. With Agent Atkins not far behind, his lips tight, they dipped beneath the yellow tape and approached a couple cops in plain clothes sipping steamy brew.

"Agent McCants. Who's in charge?"

"Myself and homicide detective Romirez. This is city jurisdiction, a state case. So what's up?"

"One of the deceased was a resident of the 10039 zoned district. Our orders are that One Federal Plaza and we're leading an investigation unit out of the 3-2 developed to monitor the criminal activities of a specific area in the city. So we're investigating all murders in, around, and associated with that zip," Trent explained.

"Okay, I read something about that unit in a union newsletter. Right now we have nothing. No expended casings, no witnesses, nothing. All we know is they were killed right after completing their shifts at the courthouse. And they were dating. He has a hole in his right cheek and a bigger one in the back of his head – entry , exit. And the woman has two holes in her. One in the torso, one in her pretty face. They made someone very angry. That's all we know right now."

"Damn," Agent Atkins huffed in disgust, reaching for the nape of his thick neck. "Nothing."

"They used revolvers. Same m.o. as the unsolved murders of Monte "Money Mont' Monanez and Donneray 'Luz' Williams," Trent McCants offered.

"I know nothing about those cases. But revolvers were definitely the weapon of choice here," detective Romirez concurred. "And all we have right now are two dead corrections officers, killed right outside the Bronx Supreme Court."

"McCants, I thought there was someone in custody for the Williams murder?" Agent Atkins pointed out.

"It's the wrong guy. The gun he was arrested with doesn't match the ballistics. And he had no gunpowder residue on his hands, according to the reports I read. They're hoping he head an accomplice, but if the suspect doesn't confirm that theory by confessing, they're gonna have to cut him loose."   Trent

McCants turned to Detective Romirez and said, "has anyone contacted the families?"

"Hey, Officer Rivera!" the bulky DT called out and a uniformed cop scurried over to the ranking lawman. "You were the first on the scene; did anyone inform the families?"

The gangly cop flipped through his notepad before saying, "Detective Leas handled that. No one was present at the fellow's home address. But the female, her younger sister was given the bad news."

As if the agents weren't listening, Detective Romirez said, "The families have been contacted."

Trent McCants checked his timepiece, saw it was almost three, and said, "We're gonna look around."

"Don't fuck up my crime scene!" Detective Romirez shouted at their backs.

Trent turned back, summoned the cop who made it to the scene first, asked, "Was there any personal property removed from the decease?"

The cop said, "As in stolen?"

"No. As in, for investigative purposes?"

"Yes. That's how we were able to contact the families."

"One family," Agent Atkins clarified.

"I should've stayed in training. Or chasing the money! Because none of this shit makes sense. I've seen enough cadavers in the last month to last me a lifetime," vented Agent McCants.

"The other night I was called to shots fired outside the Savoy Nightclub, and it turned out to be a triple homicide. In two years, I've seen my share. But these two here, cold blooded," Rivera shared, this grim look on his face. "You guys take it easy."

"One second. Does that say...West 143th Street, 9-C?" asked Trent, having caught a glimpse of the chicken scratch in the cop's notepad.

The cop took a quick gander. "Yes, it does."

That was like a hard punch to Trent's abdomen.

"What?" Agent Atkins quizzed.

"Nothing." Trent wanted to share his hunch, tell his partner he'd been in that building before to pick up his daughter back in late '87. But it was too early, and though no coincidence, so circumstantial. "Let's get downtown to the dine, see what those cameras caught."

EIGHT

Apartment 9-C was the quietest it had been in ears. You could hear a roach pissing on the rug. No music, all five TV's were off, the curtains were shut tight, the safety chain secured the door, and all the lights were out. Tyanna Jenkins had slept the entire day away, praying that when she awoke her only sister would be standing over her talking about the latest Jimmy Choo's, to the newest Ellen Tracy design, or some crazy shit that went on at the courthouse. But it was the real deal, and a reality she had to come to grips with. Shyann was a memory/

It was about 8:40 P.M. when Tyanna finally found the strength to get out of Shyann's king size bed and trudge into the bathroom. With each step, she wondered if her mother still lived at the same address on the Grand Concourse she last knew of. And if she did, whether she deserved to be notified of her daughter's death.

Tyanna remembered being nine when that lady left them for some cat she'd just met and started selling pussy for, leaving Shyann, fifteen at the time, with the responsibility of raising her. It was rough at first, they had their shortcomings, and most of their meals were stolen, but Shyann rose to the occasion. There were concerned tenants in the building who wanted to contact the Bureau of Child Welfare, seeing the girls growing so fast – not just physically, but socially – however, turned the cheek feeling it wasn't their business. The apartment experienced mad traffic, hustlas and thugs frequenting like it was a strip club. It was Capri who'd shut that down, having grown up with the girls. Still, by the time Tyanna was thirteen, this pretty girl had breasts that were large and full, eyes that held a dreamy aura, and she was very fond of boys. She also knew what they wanted, so by fourteen she'd been deflowered by some young player who hit it and ran, making her very bitter for a long time.

She recalled Shyann sights being set on Capri since he could fight and had that bully bravado to go with the good looks that made bad boys so irresistible. But when he didn't reciprocate, Shyann got pregnant a couple times by this older cat, and quickly aborted. Nevertheless, through all the trial and error, the abandonment and uncertainty, both sisters graduated high school with honors and plans to one day escape the ghetto. Now that would never happen.

In just some panties and a bra, Tyanna ran her manicured fingers through her naturally curly mane as she glared into the mirror, just long enough to find the will to keep on moving. She brushed her pearly whites, gargled, splashed a little water on her face, took another gander, then pulled her panties down and sat on the commode. When the sound of water breaking water ceased, she took a shower. as the steamy water raced down her Parkay flesh, rinsing away the suds, she remembered throwing Bones out after the bearer of the bad news broke her heart. "Don't touch me! Just leave! Now!" she had clamored sending him off furious.

Along with the scent and the overnight perspiration, she washed away the sorrow. And by the time she squeezed into her Parasol jeans and halter top, she had regained some strength. And after sliding on her pink Air Max 95s, she had an idea of who might be responsible for her sister's murder. With her makeup and hair in tact, satisfied with her appearance, she grabbed her Coach bad and hit the streets with an agenda.

Downstairs on 143rd Street Bones had his Benz wagon

parked curbside with the trunk popped, blasting Touch Me, Tease Me. In his presence was Diamond and Purple, two project chicks always on the grind, giving the young don the praise he craved after being dissed and dismissed by his girlfriend. Donned in the lastest Jordan's, some crisp Pepe jeans and a Falcons jersey, he basked in the adoration. But it wasn't the car or his appeal that had the young ladies fascinated. It was the new gray chain hanging from his neck, the icy charm at his crotch. And the bright light of the street lamp he stood beneath just enriched the jewels even more. Initially they thought it was silver like his charm until he checked them saying, "This platinum baby. Five grand worth. With the H-classes in the piece, ten stacks!"

While trying to conceal her affinity for him, Purple checked his shines and said, "Ballin'!"

Grinning, Bones nodded thinking of the gift he planned to give himself for his eighteenth birthday. Just that quick it had gone from a trip to Puerto Rico with Tyanna, to a threesome.

Due to the insane demand for Zest and Capri's product, he'd been selected to oversee things while the big homies were down in sunny Florida. Basically break brinks down to their very last compound, then feed the block. And though he had a few things of his own going on already in Pennsylvania, and always considered himself that nigga, this assignment gave him a power he'd never felt before. That is until Tyanna pulled that stunt the night before. Now the feeling was back as he got loose with his hands, touching Diamond's round tush and receiving no protest. He may've been light in the ass, but at that moment the world was his oyster.

Diamond, the teen mom of one, was one of those hustling chicks who looked good in everything she wore. But that day she looked extra good, and Bones was ready to give the shapely shortie the rest of the day off…with pay.

From a short distance Tyanna saw the whole thing. That smile on his face, the charm in his swag, his eyes on her boobies. Bones didn't give a fuck though, at least not at the time. In fact, he wanted to know if Diamond looked as good naked as she did in that skirt and heels. He had Diamond right where he wanted her, blushing and giggling. Just as he touched the tattoo on his neck, Purple said, "Here come Tyanna."

Diamond took a step back. "Uh-ooh."

Bones grabbed her by the elbow, pulling her closer, said, "I was saying…"

Tyanna was moving with a purpose. It started with the intentions of apologizing to Bones, then explaining what'd happened though she knew where his allegiance lied. Now it was the sight of Bones' mouth near Diamond's ear and his hand on her waist that had Tyanna's strut looking so fierce.

"Excuse me Diamond, but umm, that be me, and I think you're a little too close. So use those last season Chanel shoes to beat it; fond some fiends to serve," Tyanna said with a slickness that even Bones couldn't front on. "And you, Bones, I come done here to talk to you, to let you know what's really good with me – and you all in her fuckin' face. What's really good with you?"

Diamond and Purple had walked off by the time Tyanna jumped in Bones' face. He wasn't trying to hear that, and showed it by not responding. She sulked, and he cleared his throat, all eyes on the young couple in turmoil. In a prudent move, Bones shut the hatch on his car, killing the music, was about to jump in and pull of when Tyanna go real silly with it. "And to think I was falling in love with your sickly ass!"

No one on the scene knew Bones battled sickle cell and diabetes, but assumingly figured it was something serious when the bling on Bones' hand ascended and came down sparkling and fast. Tyanna never saw the vicious smack coming or going. All she heard was the impact and felt the sting, and could only imagine the redness that would be left behind on her light skin. Mouth agape, she jogged off holding her face trying to escape the hooting and hollering. Everybody that was out there that night watched as she jetted into Christine's building. Bones wanted to follow her, wanted to apologize, console her, but instead he dropped his head, got in his car and peeled off. He was at a traffic light in disbelief when Tyanna crossed the threshold of Christine's apartment.

"Hey," she said speaking to the lady of the house, her girlfriend, and daughter.

Mecca immediately noticed the redness on Tyanna's jawline and neck and asked, "Everything alright?"

Looking for no sympathy, Tyanna returned, "Allergies."

Mecca knew better, having experienced her share of domestic abuse, but reclaimed her seat and said. "Tina's in her room."

Christine was listening to music while straightening up when she heard Tyanna call her name. "Ty, what happened? You all right, gurl?" she asked after seeing Tyanna's face. "Who hit you?"

"Nobody," she lied, perching herself at the foot of the bed, sinking deeper into sorrow, then came the tears. "Tina, they killed my sister. Shyann is gone."

"Nooooo," Christine bemoaned, forgetting all the hating Shyann had been doing and took a seat next to Tyanna.

"Some detectives came to the house one this morning. They wanted me to come identify the body."

"Want me to go with you?" Christine offered, gently stroking Tyanna's forearm. "I'll go with you."

"No. I know it's her; she didn't come home last night. Didn't call to say she was staying out or anything. And when I paged her, she didn't call back. I don't wanna she her like that."

"Why would somebody do something like that?"

"Don't know," Tyanna sulked. "Where Pri at?"

"Miami. Why what's up?" Christine quickly replied, her slanted eyes checking Tyanna's demeanor.

Miami???, Tyanna mused, lifting her head. By the time her eyes met Christine's, she thought of that slick shit she heard

71

Shyann say to Capri the last time he was at their apartment. "…And if I don't start getting it, you won't be giving it to nobody," resounding in her mind. What Shyann was mad about, she didn't know. But she knew Capri was a wild boy, capable of making Shyann disappear, and that onto itself was enough to make her case even though he had an alibi.

"What about Zest?"

Christine said, "You have to ask his girl, your dude's sister Princess."

Hearing Bones name made Tyanna reach for her face, and hated men. Her eyes dropped to the top two undone buttons on Christine's coochie cutter shorts.

"Why you asking about them anyway?"

"Did he mention anything to you about the conversation he and my sister had that nigh y'all came to my crib?"

"I did ask him what they were talking about and he said some jailhouse politics. Why?"

"Forget it," Tyanna stammered in a stank tone that didn't sit well with Christine.

"And why you looking at me like that?"

"What you mean?"

"You know what I mean! And it's making me uncomfortable."

Tyanna moved closer, her dreamy but teary eyes more lecherous than anything now. "I never wanna make you uncomfortable. You all I got now. You know that, right?"

Christine was taken aback, based on the fact that they hadn't been the best of friends since she met Capri, and far more surprised when Tyanna tried to kiss her. "What are you doing?!" she snapped.

Tyanna didn't respond, just grabbed Christine's shoulders and tried again, this time harder.

"Bitch! If you don't get off me!" Christine sneered, shoving Tyanna with every ounce of power her 140-lb frame could muster.

"Look who's acting brand new again," Tyanna chided in disbelief. "First you get on some new shit when this nigga come around. And now look at you."

"I don't know what the fuck you talking about."

Tyanna rose to her feet. "Wasn't you the one with the curiosity? The one who wanted to see what it was making your mother so happy after you got shitted on all crazy by that kid from Macombs Road?"

Those weren't inquires, they were reminders that cut deep. Christine had initiated the try-sexual shit. Touched Tyanna one drunk night in the right place after a party, and fell asleep fulfilled. They came together a couple other inebriated nights – then it was like it never happened. Now, more than a year since the curiosity, she was struggling to keep Tyanna's hands from her panty line.

Tyanna didn't just see a warm body to kiss and coddle with, or a bosom to cry in. she saw a 5-foot-7 mocha beauty with silk for hair, skin that looked like she bathed in Palmer's Cocoa Butter and luscious-ness she wanted to unfold on.

"Ty, stop!" Christine demanded.

"Just kiss me like you did—"

"No! I was curious, not—"

"I know. Not gay. Neither was I! until you. But when you needed me, it was all good," Tyanna said backing off. "You're so full of shit. Just like that nigga that got ya head all fucked up. He don't give a fuck about you. All he care bout is his self. And you sitting up in here being faithful."

Feeling a bit hypocritical, Christine said, "Ty, you don't understand."

"Understand what? You don't understand! But you did when we was strapping on and fucking the shit out of each other, with your mother and Monica's equipment!"

"Tyanna!"

"What?"

"Get the fuck out of my house, before I fuck you up. And

don't you ever in your life disrespect me like that. Leave!"

Tyanna's eyes welled up again. This time the tears spilled uncontrollably leaving dark streaks from the mascara. As she watched yet another door shut in her life, she grabbed her handbag and advanced towards the bedroom door. But before leaving she turned back. "I finally see you for who you really are. A selfish bitch. A wannabe! I hope that nigga shit all over you! Put babies in you and leave your ass for dead!"

"You wished that long before today. And I knew it. You were hating the day I met him. You and your sister, you conniving stunt!"

Tyanna stormed out the room rolling pass everyone in the front room, straight ignoring their voices. Did the same thing to her crew and counterparts trying to show concern when she got downstairs. Even ig'd Bones who'd spun the block looking for her.

A livery cab pulled up on 7th Avenue and some tall dark skinned kid hopped out. Tyanna got right in that same cab and told the driver, "Featherbed Lane in the West Bronx, ahk!"

"You know the guy who just got our?" the cabby fished heading for the Harlem River Drive.

"Nope, why?"

"By Allah, I jus' pick that guy up from Featherbed Lane."

"don't know him, just a coincidence," Tyanna retorted, the only thing on her mind being revenge.

NINE

More tapes, more chalk, more lawmen and more forensic experts, thought Trent McCants as he sidled over the scene of yet another unwitting victim of senseless violence. Richie Rich had two holes in his chest, one in his face and two in his right forearm. Having avoided all verbal interaction by brandishing his shield, Trent began soliciting information on the corner of this on-way street. Immediately he noticed all the windows of the restaurant were still in tact, not a bullet hole in sight. He then noticed several available parking spots, something that is very rare in the city that never sleeps. And particularly where the lifeless lay twisted. With a quick glance he was able to tally two dozen spent casings on the opposite side of the street.

Agent Atkins said, "He was a target."

Trent didn't respond, noticing the evidence of returned fire in the brick wall just a few feet from the spent casing. He trekked across the street where the diner was located, turned back and fixed his green eyes in the area he'd just left. "This unfortunate fellow wasn't alone. He was with a shooter."

Together they searched for potential evidence of any others being wounded, hoping for some good ole' DNA. But nothing conclusive lead them to the front door of the diner where they were met by the general manager, a portly and balding man who appeared to've been just removed from slumber. While wiping cold from his puffy eye, he promptly directed the agents to the manager of third shift personnel, a slender man with a paunch for a stomach who appeared to be juggling thoughts.

"What can you tell me about the events of tonight, sir?" Agent Atkins questioned/

"...All I know is it was very busy, then there was an outburst, then things quieted down, then as soon as they left, the shooting started out there leading to mayhem in here," the third shift manager replied searching his pockets for something.

"And who did you see?"

"Two different hip hop crews," he said, shoulders hunched, lighter in one hand, cigarette in the other.

"And what makes you think they're hip hop crews?"

"The cars, the clothes, the jewelry."

"And what do you remember most about these crews besides the cars, the clothes, the jewelry?"

"All the traffic. I mean, every time one left, another arrived. And the guy who seemed to be calling the shots was tall with a big chest and big shoulders, a handlebar mustache—"

"Action!" Trent exploded shocked that the overload could be placed at the scene of a murder.

"—and the other guy, a light skinned male. The look I saw in his eyes I haven't seen since I was a youth back in my native Poland."

"And what was this look?"

"Like he could kill and not think twice about it. He had his baseball cap very low, but I could still see his eyes, and the cut running across his right cheek. There was a lot of pain in those eyes too."

"was he the shooter?" Atkins asked, urgency in his posture. "Did this man with the handlebar fire a gun?"

A lump formed in Trent's throat.

The manager looked towards his now empty restaurant, spent nicotine streaming from his narrow nostrils. "No, he sat right there eating apple pie, watching with his entourage while the shooting happened."

Trent released as sign, not sure if it were relief or resentment that Capri wasn't fingered. And then the manager said, "And the other guy, he didn't shoot neither. Someone shot at him, and like he was a godfather, he was covered up and rushed to a car and raced off."

"Can I see the tapes?" Trent asked knowing that would be their only chance of furthering their investigation right now.

"Patrick, come! Take these men to the back and show them the tapes!"

They were led to the rear of the diner, where they were eventually told, "Somebody forgot to turn the recorder on."

TEN

Capri couldn't remember Action's beloved princess ever looking better. Every tress of her long dark mane was in place. Her eyes were slanted just like Christine's, but shaped like almonds with glowing brown orbs. Her lips were pouty, and her teeth were a thing of perfection – thanks to the work of braces. With the height of her miscreant father, and the beautiful curves of her introverted mother, she was a physically blesses specimen. Round tits, profound hips, and a mount od ass.

But then again, prior to that sunny afternoon Capri had always viewed her as a sibling, making her off limits to him and anyone he knew. Now, like a luscious piece of forbidden fruit, the five-foot-eight PYT was ripe for the taking. Capri couldn't believe his luck when that white J30 pulled up alongside his 850i at a traffic light on 125th Street. He hit his horn, and they made eye contact. "Pull over right there, Madison Ave, by A Taste of Seafood," he urged forcing a smile.

Grinning and giddy, she said something to her passenger, then veered to her right. Not only did she park up, but she hopped out and ambled over, her passenger not far behind before he was parked.

Zest was in the passenger seat of the 850i, and in a low pitch suggested they bound her pretty little wrists and mouth with duct tape, stick her somewhere safe, send Action a ransom note, and if the demand wasn't met pronto, slip one of those pretty little toes she had peeping out her Prada pumps and leave it at one of Actions establishments. But Capri had grander ideas, something so sinister that even he began to wonder was he losing his mind.

"I see you back in Harlem, huh?" he had sent Katrina's way when she got to his window.

She spoke to Zest first, receiving a head nod from him, then said, "Why shouldn't I be? I'm from Harlem just like you."

"After that incident at the Lux games, your father came through with the Action Pack, and shut the block down. Oh yeah, and he ran up in a crib or two, I believe. You don't think that made some people mad?"

Her body was tightly bound in a sexy black cat suit, and Capri was looking tight at the cleft where her legs connected when she said, "I didn't think he would get that angry when I told him about it. He's usually so kind and sweet. But then again, I am the fruit of his loins. And which one of them bitches giving you face anyway? Christine or Tyanna?"

"I don't kiss and tell," Capri told her on some real smooth shit, one hand on his crotch, the other on the wheel. And while she was digesting his elusive response, he said, "I'm shooting out to Miami, 'sup you try'na go do it wild big with me?"

"Wild big?" she grinned.

"I will be twenty-three next week."

"For how long?"

"About a week."

"I gotta see if it's okay with my father."

"How old are you now? Nineteen?"

"Eighteen, going on nineteen."

"You're old enough to be making your own decision now, Trina."

Something about that statement didn't rest well with Katrina. Mainly because she couldn't believe Capri was encouraging her to defy her parents. Yet, she chose to ignore Capri's obvious disregard for Action's authority instead of becoming suspicious. Having enjoyed the fruits of her father's treachery all her life, Katrina pretty much wanted for nothing, and shoed her gratitude with obedience and never transgressing. But there was something missing, and that something happened to be relevance some place other than home, somewhere other than with family. And as of lately she'd been having this secret craving for a small morsel of the streets and its many extremities. So it was no surprise to her when she said, "Let me think about it."

Iris said, "What's there to think about?"

Capri's eyes averted to the unfamiliar voice with the sultry undertone, checked her out for a little minute then nodded.

"Did I hear anybody ask Iris anything?" Katrina retorted in a voice tinged with jealousy, her eyes tightening like a wild cat looking to intimidate.

"I'm not really her brotha, Iris, but I am in agreement. What's there to think about?" said Capri playing the BFFs against each other while wondering what shorty's ethnicity was. He remembered her coming to one of the basketball games over the summer, but didn't recall her resembling a Brazilian bombshell. "What up, you try'na go?"

"When are you leaving?" Iris quickly quizzed, so excited Capri could see her nipples began to press against the soft cotton of her tight baby T-shirt.

"Today, right after I put a few things in motion," said Capri in a tone so slick that even he had to smile.

"Should I pack or, will doing it wild big entail a shopping spree?" Iris murmured, licking her full lips and grabbing her shapely hips nearly stealing the show from the boss lady of their clique.

Capri said, "It's gonna be so hot down there, we may not even need clothes."

"You make it sound so tempting," Katrina mused, ambling right pass Iris and closer to Capri's car, her proud papa the last thing on her mind for the very first time. Though, she couldn't forget that distraught look on his face as she passed him earlier that morning on her way out.

It was late August, and the city was experiencing a record low on the heat index, but just that quick it was beginning to feel like the summer was just beginning.

Action sat at the head of his table under massive stress, him narrowly escaping that barrage of bullets on his mind. On top of that, the fact that Destro was found in Brooklyn cooked to a crisp, half his skull gone, just wasn't sitting well. Action felt anemic. Had been that way since an old buddy with a shield delivered the news. The evidence against the people responsible was scant, but that wouldn't stop Action from finding guilt and sentencing cats to death. He felt he had to immediately strike back to protect his reputation.

"I don't know about you niggas, but I'm sick!" he said to no one in particular. And before anyone replied, he added, "We're the guerrillas of this shit!" What he really meant was they were the gargantuan! Key word: Were.

Zac said, "He didn't deserve to go out like that."

"Damn right he didn't!" Action scoffed. "And somebody knows something!"

"Nobody's talking, boss," Mumbles mumbled.

Brother Joe was there too, his swat cap low, his dark beard sharp as a Gem Star blade fresh out the box. With that tooth missing from the front of his mouth, the short and stout man said, "You know Destro's car was discovered in Queens with some seventeen year old dame dead in the front seat, shot to death? For the simple fact that his body was found in BK, and the car in Q-Borough, I think it was some Uptown cats."

Action reached for his shaven face, kneaded with a purpose – to slow down that headache that was coming on with a vengeance – before saying, "When Destro told me he despised the same people I despise, oppose all those who oppose me, I

81

knew he was my friend. So, since we have no clue who's responsible for this, the last person he had a dispute with dies."

"Boss, that'll be like trying to find a needle in a hay stack. He was well respected out there, and even more feared," Mumbles again mumbled.

"Find somebody!"

Both Zac and Mumbles nodded.

"And what about the Porsche pushing punk who, who pulled that trigger last night?" Action went on to say.

Brother Joe said, "I handled that."

Everyone at the table looked at each other.

When Brother Joe got his hands dirty it usually resulted in a closed casket. Once he'd shot a fool so many times, the victim's clothes cought fire. Another time a victim was discovered stuffed in his safe after two days of death polluting the air forced neighbors to notify authorities. He'd jig you in the jugular, bash your brains in with anything he could get his hands on, toss you on the third rail, off a rood, out a moving car; didn't matter so long as were no longer existing. There was just no method to his madness. And most of the time cats never saw it coming.

So they all wondered how this one went down. And curbing their curiosity, Brother Joe said, "Piano wire wrap around the neck. Didn't want to wake his lady and kids."

Action picked up a framed photo, an eight-by-ten of he and Destro out in Vegas offering gold bottles of champagne to the camera. It was obvious the pain he was feeling was complex and unsettling, and almost overwhelming. While Action was mourning, eyes a bit misty. Brother Joe was witnessing weakness. How could a grown man cry?, he wondered as Action said, "When things settle down we'll do something in memory of him, since all they left us was his skeleton." He then turned to a small table behind them where bills of all denominations sat neatly. "And make sure his family wants for nothing."

"Anything else?" asked Mumbles.

"Yeah, did you take care of Nickels yet?"

"Zac was supposed to handle that?" Mumbles spat out.

Zac felt betrayed, but there was too much going on for internal beefs, so he rose to his feet and said, "I'm on that right now."

Mumbles said, "Zest is nowhere to be found. I followed Princess for about an hour earlier this morning to Central Park West, which is where I'm sure he's staying too."

"And where Capri?"

"Nobody's seen him," Zac quickly spat out hoping to never cross paths with the ticking time bomb.

Action witnessed the uneasiness in his cohort as Zac spoke of Capri, and was about to spaz out when he was disturbed by an incoming call. As he lifted the phone from its cradle his eyes were all over Zac. He rose so quick, so swiftly, so angered that his chair slid about two feet back. And shaking his head, he gave them his back. "Hello! What? When? Nahhhh," lamented Action, and it wasn't missed by his crew members. Moments later he slammed the receiver back on its cradle, then told them, "The video rental, the furniture warehouse, my car dealership, and the salon are all on fire right now! And some cats came through and shot up Tremont Avenue too. Professor and Satin are dead."

Not one of the men in his sight could believe what had fallen on their ears, as their eyes bounced from one another in this slow sedated state. Just the day before they were throwing their weight around, the titans of takedown. Before the Midnight Express Diner fiasco, their affairs were in order and the world seemed to be at their feet.

In a matter of hours the tables had rotated.

The pendulum of power had shifted.

They'd all witnessed Action's rise, were even instrumental in the success, and were now witnessing the potential debacle. Before anyone could offer a sentiment, Action was back on the phone. "You sure?"

"Yeah, boss. Pro's dead. And Moe just drove Milk to the hospital. I don't think he's gonna make it though. His intestines were hanging, about twenty feet worth. Never seen no shit like that man."

"What the fuck happened?"

"Some young bucks in black fatigues with red bandannas over their faces came through with street sweepers, letting them go. They sprayed the entire arcade up. Sidewalkers were hit and all. And the lounge—"

"Nah man, not my lounge?" sulked Action, his less masculine side on display.

"The lounge, boss. Cocktail bombs."

"My goddamn lounge too?" Action thought of the renovation he'd just had done. Twenty grand worth. Outdoor deck. Indoor-outdoor fireplace. The barista bar running through the center of the lounge, with tables on each side and seats at the bar itself. "Nah, man! I'm coming through there right now!"

"It's inferred hot. Feds is crawling like bedbugs."

"Sheeit!"

Action paced for a minute, the room quieter than a law library at Columbia University, all of Action's men moving about aimlessly. He reached for the remote, his mouth poked out, hit the power button and found Fox 5. A commercial. Then the talk of the town.

Boston Road, where he had invested in most of his real estate, was on the screen, infested by flames and smoke. The bomb squad, the fire department, cop cruisers, ambulance and onlookers were all he could see. Some reporter was giving the summery of her young career. But there were no leads on the brazen thugs responsible, or a motive.

Arms folded across his chest, Brother Joe said, "We're under attack."

"Ever heard of collateral damage? Casualties of war?" Action seethed, his teeth clenched like they were wired shut.

"Only in war movies," offered Zac, paying close attention to his leader's every move.

With his fist clenched in frustration, brows furrowed, Action said, "Open up some fuckin' heads, don't matter who it is. That's collateral damage. They'll be casualties of war. And make sure anybody who is somebody knows it's our work. That should buy us enough time to neutralize this shit."

Mumbles ad Zac, thinking of the fastest way to please their boss, took to the streets, pistols fully loaded and already cocked, Zest and Nickels at their focal points.

Brother Joe jumped on his phone and whispered, "Listen here baby, I ain't coming home tonight."

And Action, with his eyes a little misty, phoned his residence to make sure all was well in Queens only to find out that his daughter had left the state without permission on some unauthorized vacation.

"Who the fuck told her—" he roared in anguish only to be cut short by his matrimonial partner.

"She's fine, Anwar," Drenae conveyed unconvincingly, as she gazed at the fascinating reflection in the mirror of her bureau staring back at her.

"And how you know this?!"

Drenae ran a set of fingers through the thick and dark silky mane surrounding her face and shoulders, told him, "I know who she's with."

"Who is she with?!"

"The girl next door."

"Iris?" he cringed.

Yes."

"When I see her, I don't see the girl next door. I see a fast ass! You see the way she dresses???"

Drenae signed, sweeping her hair back over her right shoulder before resting and securing the phone there. Iris was Latina, and owned a very mature body and mind, but she came from a good upbringing, so Drenae wasn't worried and tired getting to the real reason for the sudden phone call.

"You sound like you're worried about something else. What's up?"

"Just worried about Katrina. You know she's at that age where they tend to wander, discover, and I don't want anyone taking advantage of her."

"Eighteen?" Drenae scoffed.

"Yeah!"

"I was eighteen when I met you. I was mindful of what I was doing," she replied, secretly admitting she did ignore many things she now wished she hadn't

"Times were different then," Action reasoned.

"She's fine. We raised a thinker, Anwar. You need to be concerned about A.J."

"He's only twelve, what do you mean Drenae?"

"Every time I turn around he's watching that movie Strapped. And he's becoming infatuated with toy guns. That's all. Your daughter's fine. Now what's bothering you? You rarely call the house phone. I was surprised when I heard your deep voice."

"Just wanted to say...I love you."

There was a pause.

Action's eyes fell shut, the sign of worriation.

And, Drenae's doe eyes widened, her beautiful reflection looking back at her in awe. She thought of the day she'd first noticed Action, and how her strolling up Amsterdam Avenue that warm day in that sultry mini dress had not stopped traffic, but caused a collision. A 560 Benz, all black, rear ended a small compact car, and when she looked up the man that would put two babies in her and change her life was in the middle of the street kicking the shit out of the driver of the compact car. His brute power turned her on, but it was the charm she would later meet that won her over. Like the guru of gratuity he gave her chocolate, roses, mind blowing sex in a penthouse suite, and the promises of giving her the world. He resembled nothing of his counterparts; the average street cats she was accustom to being approached by and seeing around. This cat was polished, smooth and powerful, like he'd been somewhere and was going places. And he should have, to an eighteen year old female. But outside of rescuing her from her abusive mother and that dilapidated apartment on 137th and Lenox Avenue, the world he promised her turned out to be her children. The house, the cars, the jewels meant nothing without his unwavering affection. She knew he had many indiscretions and many mistresses. Still, she loved him. But...she wasn't in love with him. And up until that day he'd only professed a love for her once. "Something's gotta be wrong," she pried, removing the phone from her shoulder, "because the last time you told me you love me, I was in labor, pushing your son out. And for as long as I've known you, love is something you never openly express."

Action was short on words, and baffled by how well his wife really knew him. Though he was a good father to Katrina and his lil' man, he'd been as faithful to his vows as a pimp to his promises, sleeping with women from all walks of life, all corners of the world, something he knew Drenae knew but never spoke on. Most of their communication pertained to their two children, and never once had he discussed his street biz with her. She knew he had very little respect for the law, that they were well off because he was very good at translating his visions into reality, but she had no idea he owned all that property on fire headlining all four New York City's news outlets.

"Yeah, you're right something is bothering me."

Drenae said, "Why the epiphany all of a sudden?"

"I'm getting old, and it's about time you start going out instead of sitting home."

"Go out? I don't even have any friends," she laughed. "My children are all I have. You made sure of that."

Action took a seat, sat silent, thinking of how far apart in the spectrum of womanhood Drenae was from the lover she replaced, Action's first choice to marry. Olivia Hayward. Because he didn't want history repeating itself, he practically sheltered her from the world making her the reclusive homebody she was. Her only joys came from her children and the occasional sexual mauling she'd received from Action when she'd least expected it.

"And you say Katrina's fine, huh?"

"She's fine and probably can't wait to get home."

Little did they know, their daughter was on the other side of the country shacked up in a one bed motel room telling Capri, "You may not know this, but champagne makes me do crazy things."

"In that case, I'm gonna fill your glass to the top," Capri returned, amazed by how well she was filling out that Burberry bikini she'd picked up about an hour before they boarded a seven o'clock flight out of Kennedy on United. "And what do you consider crazy, Trina?"

"Promise you won't look at me different, and I'll tell you" she insisted, looking back over her shoulder checking to see if Iris was still in the bathroom changing.

Capri poured himself a glass, said, "I'm the last person to be passing judgment."

She gave him this precarious gaze, took a taste of her bubbly, slowly swallowed, then licked her lips before saying, "Well, I'm still a virgin, but after a couple glasses of Moet, I've gone down on a couple guys at school."

Capri had the bottle to his lips when those words left hers, and almost as if volcanic, champagne burst from his mouth finding Katrina's face ruining not only the moment but her mascara and blush. Capri expected her to be embarrassed, or on edge, but she was far from that. In fact, she found the whole thing to be funny, and chimed, "I see somebody can't hold their liquor."

"That's my fault," he said in a charming delivery that just made Katrina all the more comfortable.

She went on to whisper back, "My face isn't the only place you got me wet," her warm breath now laced with the sweet scent of Chandon.

Missing the sexual innuendo the young ingénue shot at him, Capri's orbs dropped to her deep cleavage.

Using the back of her hand, she wiped her face and said, "Not there, silly. Between my legs."

Immediately Capri felt the heat. That surge of electricity that transforms manhood from flaccid to fullness. Just to see how she would react, Capri loosened his belt and button fly, freeing the erection. At first Katrina was paralyzed by its size. And then with this competitive nature, she stuck her glass out for more champagne before removing her bikini top.

Up until that day Capri was under the impression that Patience had the prettiest tits he'd ever seen. But like everything else in his life, that too had changed. Salivating at the mouth, his eyes were transfixed on the twins. He took in the splendor as the gentle breeze coming off the beach front and through the open window stiffened her nipples adding to the surrealism of the whole notion for them both.

Licking her lips in delight, Katrina said, "You gonna pour me some more Mo' or what?"

Capri filled her back up, then sat the bottle down and took her into his grasps with a roughness that she cozied up too. The caress of his hands was unbelievable to her; and she sipped away cheesing. Like her father, she was good at bringing visions to reality, but even she didn't see this one coming.

Amazed by the beauty of her melons, he slowly dragged the tips of his fingers over her right breast, following the shape and the contour. Then moved to the left. They were super soft, full and firm, the exact same color as the rest of her brown sugared flesh. He palmed them, sucking on her nipples until they were so hard the slightest touch sent sensation through Katrina's whole body. Her eyes held a dreamy aura. And there was this ultra-sense of sensuality coming off of her as she moaned, finishing off that second glass.

With a lot of tongue they began to kiss passionately, like they were long standing lovers. She dropped her top and the glass on the bed, and a freakiness and promiscuity he could've never predicted emerged. She dropped low and rubbed her face up against his penis like she was a cat and his dick were a leg, then gave him her eyes before taking a taste of the pre-cum oozing from the tip. In the blink of an eye, half his dick was in her mouth, drool slipping from the corner of her agape mouth. And she knew exactly what she was doing.

As much as he loved getting head, and as great as it was feeling, busting her open was really where his mind was. And when better than while her girlfriend was in the shower? He lifted her to full stance, reached for her bottoms and pushed them down over her round hips. "Wait!" she said abruptly.

"What?!" he shouted, scaring her a bit.

"For Iris."

Almost on cue, Iris emerged from the bathroom wearing absolutely nothing, skin glistening and smiling. "I like champagne too!"

She too had dropped some cash on scads of swimsuits and sexy garments before boarding the flight south. Capri had visions of seeing her in it all, but didn't recall thoughts of catching her in nothing so soon. And was rather surprised by how comfortable she was with her sexuality. It was like Katrina wasn't even there.

Taking in her beauty, he got her a glass. "Here you go, sexy lady."

Iris downed her bubbly like her throat was a drain, her eyes fixated on the engorged member protruding from the fly of Capri's jeans the whole time. Simpering, she said, "Yeah, y'all ain't really related, huh?"

Capri's eyes were all over her. The mango sized tits with the honey gold nipples. That juicy heart shaped ass. Her flat tummy, small waist and the flaring from it. That camel toe

90

between her thighs with the Brazilian finish. Thanks to the 360 spin she did for his viewing pleasure.

"As related as a slave to his master," Capri returned, turning to Katrina. "Ain't that right?"

"Though I love you like a brother, I'd rather be your lover," said Katrina stepping out of her bikini bottoms.

Capri turned to iris. "What about you? What's your angle?"

"Well, actually, I'm tired of being on the outside looking in. I see it on the news, I read it in the papers, I hear it from Trina. And I find it to be so alluring!"

"What is that?"

"That shit that makes a girl's soul burn slow."

"You lost me," he shot out the side of his mouth.

"Gangstas!"

"She wants you too, Pri," Katrina interjected.

"What were you doing prior to making such a drastic decision, one that could change the natural course of your life?" Capri asked Iris.

"Taking a short term college program in the field of medical billing administration. Got one more year to go. Upon completion, I planned to travel the world with my trust fund serving as my guide," she shared, showing no sign of shyness.

"You sure you ready to leave that for this type of lifestyle?" Capri quizzed, posting up beside her and palming her ass.

"Is an ox's tail beef?" Iris chimed, embracing Capri's grasp.

The last time he befriended a chick so oblivious to the underworld and free from corruption, her name was Patience McCants. And it was one of the best moves he'd ever made. "If there's ever anything you can do for me, just let me know," he said chuckling, though there was a seriousness in that statement that both women could feel.

"How about I do something about that erection," Iris replied, Katrina in the corner of her eye.

"Do as you see fit," Capri shot back, taking a seat at the foot of the bed where Katrina was perched watching their whole exchange.

Iris ambled over, her face full of mirth, and curtsied, lowering her head towards Capri's dick. She grabbed him with both hands, brushed her lips against the tip, kissed it a couple times, then licked a little before sucking him off lovely. Capri watched intently, every muscle in her mouth being used to delivered ultimate sensation. Pushing her hair to the side, he was able to see her slippery lips slide up and down his shaft, turning him on even more as the feeling intensified. With him now hot and bothered, her saliva all over his manhood, she left him and crawled over to Katrina. She parted her legs and leered at her BFF's pussy thinking of the very first time they got this close. Katrina was already wet from the attention Capri had bestowed upon her lovely tits, too remembering their first encounter which was just a few weeks ago after a steamy game of truth-or-dare. Now she was ready to add dick to the equation.

Iris licked and lapped at Katrina's inner thighs before slithering her tongue inside her slippery pussy and all over every inch of her inner and outer labia. When Iris began to blow softly on the clitoris, Katrina nearly lost her mind, chiming, and grinding her preciousness all over Iris's tongue. With her tits now in her hands, Katrina squeezed painting, unable to hold back what was about to come. She came squirting her creamy orgasm all over Iris's pretty face.

Both, the least embarrassed, looked at each other and giggled.

To return the favor, Katrina put Iris on all fours, ass high, spreading her cheeks apart. She stuck her tongue as far as she could into Iris' vagina before adding two fingers, swiftly stimulating her best friend, sending her into a frenzy. In no time Iris murmured "Ooohmigod!"

Capri watched lusting, and was about to bogart shit and just start stabbing them with his dick, when Iris cried, "I'm cumming!"

The shriek halted him. And as Iris shook violently,

Katrina's face still in her puss, Capri stood up.

After their orgasms and almost as though they were on the clock, both ladies scampered over to Capri and fixed their lips on his anxious dick. Capri exhaled as Iris slobbed the dick while gently jerking him off. His hand found Katrina's doobie, wrapped some of her tresses around his fist and took to her hungry mouth, plowing back and forth while Iris attended to his testicles, lapping away like they were honey roasted.

When he'd had enough of their mouths, he tossed Katrina on the bed and took her doggy style, his manhood ripping her insides. Face buried in the sheets, she cried out in agony. To her it felt like she was going to die. To him, it was the tightest situation he'd ever been in, and didn't want to pull out. But he did, telling her to about face as he jerked off. Just as her face met his crotch, he ejaculated, splashing all over her misty face. When he was done spewing on her, he slapped her with his dick. Hate wasn't a strong enough word for what he felt for her father the man who killed his parents. The man responsible for the young lady at his feet's very existence. He slapped her with his dick again, told her, "Go clean your fuckin' face while I see what Iris is working with."

That wasn't exactly how Katrina envisioned being spoken to after getting split for the very first time. She knew he wouldn't wrap her in his arms and thank her for giving him her virginity, but at least an earnest showing of appreciation would've been cool. Not only was her feelings hurt, but he'd gotten jizm in her hair. A little distraught and disoriented, she did as she was told. And when she returned hoping to smooth things over with her first, like a sexy cat, Iris was crawling over to him. She licked at the slit in his dick, wrapped her lips around it, and in seconds he was hard again. Katrina stood off and watched what transpired next. Capri was busting Iris' ass. Literally. He'd decided to take a note out of Li'l Kim's book, and put it in Iris's butt. She had no idea he was going to do that, and Katrina watched wondering how he could even fit into her anus. The expression on Iris' face

PART II

ELEVEN

"So, when you go' handle that, Tack?"

"Soon. I gotchu. What's his name again? Dupri?"

"No! I said Capri, nigga!! And you been tellin' me you gon' handle that for you for two days now!!" Tyanna beamed, as she watched the big fella count away at his big chips.

"Slow up! You fuckin' my count up! I gave you the money for ya sister's funeral, right?"

Tyanna looked around the cozy apartment, dreading the idea of being there. "Yeah! But…"

"So what make you think I ain't gon' handle that for you?! And how the fuck you know he killed her?!"

She had nothing concrete, just capability, motive, and speculation. But she expected immediate relief, thinking a nigga was suppose to get up, and go kill at will, without confirmation. "I just know!"

"Hol' up! Hol' the fuck up! I don't see you for like two months! Don't know what you was doin'. Or who you was fuckin'. And when I do see you, you come Uptown, tellin' me you want a nigga killed!"

Tack was doing some nice things up in the Bronx. He and his clique were flipping a couple bricks a week, and clientele was increasing by the day. It would've took him nothing to send some shooters through to lay a target down, but he had no intentions of moving to Tyanna's accord.

"I was goin' through something. I needed some time away to make sure being with you is what I really want. And it's you I really want," she lied, with a straight face.

"Ya lil' yellow ass..." he hesitantly laughed, then continued, "...tryna run that weak ass game! You lucky I got love for you! But I don't believe shit you just said! It's all good though."

Tyanna smiled at the sucka-for-love, as she picked up his daughter. Deep inside, she couldn't stand the little girl, at times even calling her ugly to her face. But to have it her way, she was willing to stomach the atrocious looking baby, just as she did Tack's fat black ass.

"Right now he in Miami with his niggas!" she, for the fifth time, murmured, then kissed his daughter's cheek. "You so cute."

"I heard you the first time you said he was outta town! What I wanna know is how the fuck he hit ya sister, if he o.t?"

"He probably did it before he left! Or had a nigga do it for him. He got niggas that move he say so."

Tack raised his brows, sensing potential drama, before saying, "You tryna start a war, lil' mama?! I'm about money, not none of that bullshit."

Tack had risen above the buggin' and thuggin', making a name for himself during the 80's. He believed the wildin' was now for the up-and-coming. But he had no problems faking it to get what he wanted. And he wanted nothing more than to capture Tyanna's heart. Little did he know, he would never possess her cold muscular organ.

"I would do it for you, boo," she insincerely bellowed, with his daughter on her hip, and her hand on the other.

He looked at his daughter, thought about her ugly-ass-mother, then shifted his sight to Tyanna. "And you just want the kid who smacked you the fuck up?"

"Yeah, I want somebody to kick his little ass!" she clamored, while trying to convince herself she no longer loved

Bones. But it would take more than fucking Tack to shake the emotional attachment she had with Bones. And she knew it was her own lack of expression that got her checked, and sent her running into Tack's arms.

"I'ma have Fame and Shaka handle that. Put her jacket on, it's chilly out there."

"Why her mother be dressin' her in this cheap shit!" Tyanna snapped. "You should let me take her shoppin'."

"She only one, she don't know no betta," Tack defensively replied. "Come on! I got some shit to do! And you gon' stop ridiculing my daughter!"

A few stories below, Tack's soldiers were bubbling and betting cash at a dice game. When they saw the big man exit the building with his red-bone cutie and youngest daughter, they shifty acknowledged him.

"Tack Head, what up baby?" one cat blurted out.

Another cat, with a vicious cut on his face, said, "The champ is here! What up, Tack? It's a couple gees in the bank."

Tack replied, "I been stop shootin' dice in the street, I take my show down to Vegas where it's a gee and up, jus' to place a bet."

"And when was this?"

"The same year I stopped shootin' niggas!"

The spectators wasted no time getting in Tack's good grace by laughing. But after seeing the scar-faced kid's grill, they piped it sown, not wanting to be added to his list of bodies.

"We all gotta start somewhere, Tack!" the kid replied to Tank's cynical remarks.

"Scarface Dave, I ain't got nothin' but love for you. We came up together, sun. And I might need you to put some work in for me!"

"I ain't cheap no more, big fella. We'll rap later," the kid Dave replied, then got back on his second grind. "Money on the wood make the game go good!"

"Bet fifty you don't four and betta!" Tack could hear as he kept it moving, stopping a few feet away to speak with his little mans.

"Shaka, what up? Fame, what's poppin' out here?"

Pretty boy Shaka popped his collar, and said, "We makin' sure it come correct! I been thinkin' about getting' another blue SC 400. Whatchu think?" with his eyes on Tyanna's thick thighs.

"For what? You already had one of those!" Tack replied.

Fame invaded saying, "I said the same shit," remembering the night they were stripped, robed, and shot at. They never told anyone, vowing to handle it themselves. But they hadn't returned to Club Esso since.

Tank surveyed the crowd standing behind his young lieutenants, and noticed another hood fella he hadn't seen in some time. "Franco, what up? When you get home?"

"How many times I gotta tell you, my name is Nitti?!! Don't nobody call me Franco no more!" the just released felon replied with deep resentment for the big fella.

"My fault, little daddy!" Tack quipped, with an ice-grill as cold as the one Nitti had on his face.

Watching the men, and listening to their unfriendly word-play, Tyanna reflected back to the night she shot up to the Bronx. She remembered the stubborn kid standing before her as the same dude that hopped out the cab on 7th Avenue. Small world, she said to herself, wondering who he was visiting in her projects.

"Come here, Nitti," Tack urged, walking towards the corner of University and 174th. Reluctantly, Nitti followed. At the phone booth, Tack said, "You did a little year and all that. But ain't nothing change since you been gone. I'm still the top dog round here. That lil' beef we had years ago, that's dead. Was a money thing, we working with respect now."

"Nigga, you told me I can't pump in my own hood," Nitti

ranted, his eyes on the towering buildings of Sedgwick Houses. "I lived around here my whole lie. This be me just as much as it's you."

"Lower you voice, I'm talking to you with respect. Now listen, I was on my bullshit back then. If you wanna get down now, it's whatever. And to show you it's all love, here."

Tack Head removed two grand from the mitt he pulled from his Avirex jacket, handed it to Nitti. Nitti took it, eyes wide looking like an alley cats in the night honing in on a fish bone. But that didn't change his mind about sending Capri in his direction. Then the entire hood would be his. So he thought.

"Good look, bee," slipped from the side of Nitti's mouth.

It wasn't just a handout, Tack really felt sorry for the kid. And it showed as he zoned in on Nitti's leaning boots and ashy jeans. He had the Bronx looking bad. "It's more where that came from. Just get at me."

"I'ma get at you!" Nitti replied, as he watched Tack walk off. He watched him leave some words with his squad. Watched as he sped off in his forest green Ford Explorer with his kid and girl. Then he strolled down the hill to Macombs Road where his baby mama lived. He stopped in the store on 172nd, grabbed a 22oz brew, two pints of Brayers, then headed towards 1515 Macombs Road. When he got on the elevator, he pulled out the mitt, counted it again and again. "There's a lot more where this came from," he laughed wishing he'd ran into that blessing just a little earlier. Then he wouldn't have looked so foul, and could've came through for his daughter with a lot more than some ice cream.

Immediately after ringing the bell, he heard – "WHO IS IT?" – almost as if his BM was expecting someone.

He said, "Nitti." And almost in the blink of an eye, she was standing there, door ajar, with her arms folded across her bust.

"Your mother told me you came home two days ago. You shoulda been came to see Ashley! And when you do come, it's after ten, and you're drinking."

103

"Where's my daughter?" he muttered, then put the bottle to his mouth.

"You lucky I just fed them," she snarled leading the way into the flat, that ass dangling from her boy shorts. "Ash, your dad's here!"

"Daddy!" the young girl cooed racing towards him.

He sat the beer down, scooped her up and swung her around, eventually bringing her in for a huge hug. "Hi baby. You miss me?"

"Yeah! You spending the night?"

Nitti looked around the nicely furnished apartment, amazed by what he saw. He put her back down, said, "Nah, mama. I live somewhere else. Here, this is for you. Give your brother one."

"Dominique!" she called out, skipping out to the rear of the flat.

"Asia, I see you doing good. New furniture. That's gangsta."

You ain't gangsta!, she thought wondering what she ever saw in him.

"It was just a compliment. You ain't gotta look at me like that," he spat, hoping she'd relax. He hadn't been with a woman in ten months, and she was looking luscious. Especially her tits busting through her beater.

"Yeah, whatever!" she said, rolling her eyes.

"Lord you know how hard I try," Nitti muttered.

"Negro please! Our daughter is three, going on four. And her entire life all you did was dig me. What have you shown her?"

"Asia, I didn't come here to beef with you."

"This ain't beef. We're talking like two civilized parents. What can she expect from you this time?"

He reached in his pocket, gave her $500. "Take her shopping, get her ready for the upcoming school year."

"For once you came through for her! Here, you go give it to her," she suggested, shoving the bills back in his hand.

"Where the fuck is the mercy—"

"Cut the biblical shit, you ain't righteous! You think the Lord wasn't watching when you beat me?! Took my money"?

Nitti apologized for his foul acts of the past, then found himself seated in the kid's room. "Dom, what's going on?"

"Nothing. Thanks for the cream," the boy replied, wishing it were his father who had visited.

Nitti could see the emptiness in the boy's eyes, and hear the sadness in his voice, so he dug in his pocket and gave the boy a Grant. Asia was watching the entire interaction. How he sat with the children, acknowledging them like a father should, and wondering how come he couldn't have displayed that side of himself when it really counted.

After about 10 minutes of watching, their eyes met, and he left his seat, asked her if he could use the phone. She retrieved the cordless, him following, and said, "Don't be calling no bitches on my phone."

In seconds it was ringing, but there was no answer on the other end. He tried again. No answer. He handed the phone back, then called for Ashley. She came racing towards him, leaped into his arms. He kissed her, put her down, then headed for the door. "I'm coming for her this weekend. Aiight?"

"I ain't got no problem with that. Just call first. My friend might be here."

"You be having niggas around these kids?"

"That's right. I'm raising them alone. And – I'm grown!"

"I'm out!" he barked, crossing the threshold.

"Wait. Where' my daughter's damn money. I seen you give Dominique something, but you ain't never gave her nuffin! And...where you staying tonight?"

"My moms spot. Why?" he responded handing her the dough.

"You can stay here. Just for tonight."

"You sure?" he asked, his dick twitching.

She nodded, this earnest look on her face, and he backed

back into the apartment. In no time he dozed off on the sofa. And about an hour later, after the kids were sleep, fully nude, Asia awoke him and led the way to her bedroom which too had a hella décor. Nitti thought he was looking at something out of an adult mad as she lay back on her elbows atop her king size bed, legs splayed. And for Asia, since her friend was out of town and she had an itch, this would have to do.

TWELVE

Flossing a Versace shirt, silk slacks and crocodile shoes, Capri looked polish. It was a step up out of his usual street attire, and a good look for his 23-rd birthday celebration. And the women flanking him were both stunning as well. Killer minis by Cavalli, Giuseppe's on their feet, reflecting the latest adaptation of Capri's movement. After being stoned for two days, with fresh hairdos, mani's and pedi's courtesy of a South Beach salon, both chicks were something to see. And Capri was actually glad their pupils were no longer glazed over, and they weren't laying on their backs naked in euphoric states. The direct effects of cock and coke. It had only been a suggestion, him sprinkling coke on his penis and letting the girls lick it off. It went from going in their mouths, to their vaginas, to going up their nostrils. It definitely wasn't something he was proud of, having taken an oath to never use dope or coke himself, but he didn't feel bad either. His objective was to break Katrina down to a mere fraction of what Action had raised her to be. The carnal overtures were just a bonus. Iris, on the other hand, just happened to be in the right place at the wrong time. Like every other female who'd been deprived pleasure, she was now marveling in the afterglow of her very first moment of defiance. Unfortunately, the more intense the hunger for pleasure, the easier it is to be led astray, to become a subservient menial succumbing to the desires and powers of her master.

As they strolled the beach front beneath a heavenly body of bright stars like they hadn't a worry in the world, drawn to his sheer personality, Katrina gazed up at him. "You look like a gangsta don, boo. I wanna have your baby," she said clinging to Capri's formidable figure.

That made him think of Christine, and their love child developing inside her belly. Made him wonder whether the heir to his throne would be a junior or a princess. Then he thought of how Action had left Christine stranded, disowning her for his own selfish reasons. On that note, he glared down at Katrina and said, "One thing at a time, babygirl."

"You look good Capri, " Iris offered, too playing him close. "You should dress like this a lot more."

"I'll try to remember that," he returned forcing a smile.

Katrina said, "I'm glad you got us out that cheap motel."

"Word!" Iris added.

Capri simply smirked.

It was his intentions to bring them into discomfort, a decision conjured just to see how far they'd let him go. How much they could take before breaking down. While Stink, Zest and the crew were ditching the crowded airport for the luxury of the Green & Blue Diamond Hotel, Capri was on the phone with directory looking for the cheapest motel in town. Cheapest as in, $10 a night.

But after two days, even he was ready to blow that Carol City crevice.

The second they arrived at the Hotel, they were met in the foyer by the concierge, and then waited on hand and foot. The luggage was sent up to the suite, right across the walk from the one Stink and Zest were staying in, and the tour began. They were treated like superstars. Access to the spa, fitness gym, Jacuzzi, the sauna. But instead of taking advantage of the many amenities, the girls spent the afternoon pestering Capri for a point to powder their noses. He had other plans though – the salon for the works, bringing them back to their charismatic indulgent selves.

Wandering casually, Capri felt this sudden buzz on his hip. When he saw the number on the little black box, he nonchalantly slipped it back onto his belt and continued listening to the girls rap about their respected lives back home and how they didn't want to return. Twenty seconds later, his sky pager was buzzing again. Same number. And then again.

"Wifie?" both girls assumed in unison.

"Nah, chick from the Boogie Down."

"Dead that chick, Iris said, giggling. "You got us now."

Concurring, Katrina said, "For the first time since I started liking boys, I don't mind sharing."

Just as a smirk formed on Capri's lips, he felt another buzz. He was about to call back and check on the bitch. But it wasn't her. It was the number from the block phone. Bones' code trailing it. He slowed his stroll, turned to face the ocean, and called right back. "What's poppin'?"

"You already know. Happy birthday, gangsta."

"Thanks. What you get me?"

"I didn't get, but—"

"I'm just fuckin' with you, scoob. What's really good though? What's the word on the streets?" Capri shot back trying his hardest not to sound deliberate in his query.

Bones' cleared his throat, said, "I got a lot of shit to tell you."

"Okay."

"First, this dusty nigga came through checking for you. Name Nitti ring a bell?"

"I know him. Good nigga. You gave him my number right?"

"He already had it. More or less though, shit done got real messy out here, Blood. Ya heard."

Again Capri disguised his eagerness when he said, "Messy how?"

"Feds been spinning the block wild heavy."

"Oh yeah? You seen the feds?"

"More or less. Black nigga with green eyes."

"Green eyes, huh?" asked Capri, certain it was Trent.

"Green Eyes. Had this lil' 21 Jump Street nigga with him. And then somebody blew Action's Boston Road spots down, and peter rolled a few of his lieutenants."

"Yeah, that's messy," Capri returned, grinning. "Anybody know what it was about? What it was over?"

"Nah! Bust it though, The Voice hopped out on 145th and bodied two cats himself. Left they bodies steaming. Word is them hard head niggas tried to go into business for themselves, and boy-boy wasn't having it. But I heard from one of the Murda Gang homies that it was over his man Destro getting' peter rolled."

"The old man boogied something hisself?"

"Yeah. And word is, he looked like he was in his prime. All head shots, big homie. I feel for them cats. Oh – and Tyanna sister got her socks rocked."

"Some day we all gotta go, "Capri snarled, wishing he could tell Bones he was behind the bombings and the murders. But the less he knew, the better off everyone would be. The older you get, the wiser you get. And with the pain he planned to bring, it was wise to bask in his secrecy.

"More or less. But I ain't try'na go yet. Eventually to my conditions, but not like that. I still got a lot of living to do, if I take care of myself properly. Ya heard."

"For sure. Where you at right now?"

"About to go meet my sister at Sylvia's. powwow with her over some barbeque ribs and corn muffins. She called me sounding mad bugged out."

"What you mean?"

Capri watched the waves brush up against the shore, the cool breeze traveling with them making his silk dance, the palm trees lean, as Bones went on to say, "I can't call it. She G'd up, so I'm sure it's nothing serious."

"You hear from Nickels?"

"Yeah. Sun chilling. I went through his block a couple days ago after that riff-raff with Tyanna, and blew it down with him. A couple Dutchies stuffed with that A-black."

""What riff-raff?"

"Peanuts, bee. More or less, she just going through it, you know, big sis being on rocks and all that. But you know I know the fastest way to a bitch's heart."

"And what's that?"

"Sincerity, bee. Twenty years from now, if a chick don't remember nothing, she'll remember sincerity. When y'all get back, I'ma get her, a couple bottles of MO, and shoot out to the Poconos."

"You pretty sharp for seventeen, lil' nigga."

"Eighteen. I'll be eighteen in a couple months, bee. But I got the mind of a O.G. from Attica."

As Capri turned away from the ocean and its currents, he noticed Katrina and Iris had some company. Zest, dressed to impress; and Stink, laced in his best. Not far away was the muscle. They'd traveled along just in case those Haitians got funny style, and too looked rather dapper. "We be back on the scene in a couple days."

"say no more. Let the homies know I send my five. And that the East is the way."

"All the time," Capri said approaching his entourage.

Immediately Zest and Stink took notice to how drawn the girls were to Capri. And as expected, they played him close all the way to the restaurant where they celebrated Capri and Zest birthday at they connect's expense. The restaurant wasn't lavish like the Hotel they were staying inn, but held a quaint feel and the food was excellent. It wasn't hard to tell the owners had a real understanding of their culture and heritage.

After the drinks, Zest, Stink and Capri made ways out onto the back deck of the eatery where Capri informed them of the happenings back east. The way he told it one would think he was reading from some sensationalized movie script. The revelations brought excitement to Zest and Stink's eyes. Then chuckles followed; a sound so sinister, only a goon could relate. They were both happy to see a smile on Capri's face as well. But in his eyes they saw much more to come. And those piercing orbs were back in the restaurant, all over Katrina.

"So who are these cats? Boobie Boys? Zoe Pound?" Capri quizzed, hands in his pockets, jiggling change.

"Nah. Some homies on the rise just like us." Stink replied, checking his wrist for the time.

Capri nodded, turned to Zest. "Call you boo. I spoke to Bones, and he said that she buggin'."

Zest lips curled up into a smile as he said, "Probably because she didn't want me to make this trip. Something about her needing me around, that she needed to know that I really want to marry to marry her. When we get back we get the women and give 'em a night to remember. Saki, sushi, the whole nine bee."

Capri shrugged, said, "I'm sure Patience wouldn't mind that."

THIRTHEEN

The Yonkers Avenue Fitness Club had just shut its door to members more than an hour ago. But the lights were still on bringing brightness to the darkened strip, and the sound system was playing louder than it would have during business hours. I'm Not Feeling You!, by Yvette Michelle was setting the tone. Inside was Patience, a mist of perspiration coating her honey gold flesh. Her heart rate doubled from the cardio and the work she'd put in on the heavy bag, something that usually relieved her of the stress, though she would've rather been having makeup sex with her lover. There wasn't a trace of fat on her lissome body, no glaring weakness in her appearance. In fact, she was what wet dreams were made of. And no doubt about it; she knew she was tough. That's why she was frustrated, fed up, and ready to entertain the frequent advances of some Wesley Snipes looking banker type cat she'd met at the fitness club some time back. After two hundred jumping jacks straight, a stretch here and a stretch there, she headed to the showers dabbing her face with a towel, exhausted but invigorated.

Though she knew it was an experiment that would fail, because she wasn't attracted to the straight and narrow and was madly in love with Capri Hayward, two minutes after showering, drying, and the squeezing into a tank top, some dark jeans and designer pumps, Patience was on the phone. After a few rings, the answering machine picked up. She said, "Hey, this is Patience. Princess, if you're there, pick up. If not, call me as soon as you get a chance. I need some advice. Thanks"

She didn't really want advice, she wanted Princess to let Capri know he was about to lose a good one.

Princess happened to be standing just a few feet from the phone, on the verge of a nervous breakdown. Eyes were filled with tears. Her heart with love. Love for two cats. Frantically, she paced back and forth. One of the men took her heart years ago and never gave it back. The other, she didn't even see it coming, and got caught up in his rapture.

"Damn man! It wasn't supposed to be like this!" she cried, her eyes on the cash centering the glass dining room table centering the dining area of their spacious Central Park West apartment. "I got too attached. And now…I can't let go!"

She began to think of her little brother's wellbeing, and the retribution he would receive for her foul act. There was no question in her mind Zest would find relief in offing him if he couldn't get his hands on her once he found out she'd skipped town with his life savings.

Back and forth, from the dining table to the terrace, she wept regretting ever telling her ex about Zest.

Then came the command of her first love, loud and clear, like he was there, in her ear. It went something like this: "You know I'm getting short. Shorter than a baby's dick. And you remember what we talked about last year, right?"

Princess had nodded, her eyes everywhere but with Bill,]

"It's time to round that paper up and blow out to North Click. Like we planned."

Holding back an abundance of tears that rainy day he had made her troop way up north to visit him, she again nodded. They were one of the only couples on the visiting floor. That's how bad it'd rained.

"This for us," he slipped into her diamond studded ear while monitoring the burly redneck at the front desk. For being as close to her as he was, his visit could've been terminated. By the chin, he lifted Princess' head and continued. "Take the paper and bounce. For us."

"For us? FOR US? Divas Galore was suppose to be for us!" her heart cried as she winced form his touch. "Robbing Zest is for you!"

"Now how much did you say the young niggas was worth>:

Hesitantly she muttered, "A little over eight hundred thousand," thinking of Zest and his crazy ass cousin. She had warned Bill on numerous occasions about their ruthlessness. Their reckless abandon. But Bill didn't believe it. To him, they were nothing more than some glorified thugs who had just run out of luck.

Bill leaned back in his chair, slid his hand over his bald head, said, "I know you ain't crying over that nigga? You knew what the deal was when you told me about him. You know he can't love you like I can. Eat that pussy like me. I know you missing that anal."

Princess thought of what her world had been like with Zest, a much younger and inexperience man than Bill. The gifts, the trips, the endless nights of lovemaking. The early morning orgasms, the flowers at her lower Manhattan office, how he actually listened when she spoke. The fact that she was able to teach him a thing or two. Their chemistry overall. And unlike Bill, she never heard about him cheating.

He was doing the damn good job loving her! By many standards.

Overwhelmed, she ran over to the glass table flailing her arms. The heap of cash tumbled through the air slowly floating to the carpeted floor. She then marched over to the bar and put a dent in a brand new fifth of Hennessy. Used the rest to wash down a half bottle of sleeping pills. Thirty minutes later the lethal combination began its attempt on her life.

Later that night, Zest returned from sunny Miami on a

natural high. He had a connect that could deliver. More bricks than he'd ever seen in his life. And he was hornier than a jack rabbit, having passed up on every piece of pussy that'd been tossed his way, and ready to lay some pipe – only to be grounded by the sight of his fiancé's body laid out on the terrace. Instinctively he pulled his gun and searched the place for intruders. With the coast clear, he jetted back to the terrace thinking Princess was dead. Having check her vitals, it was clear she was only unconscious. For the first time in a long time he didn't know what to do. Seeing his cash littering his pad had his movement a little stagnant, and his mind roaming. Naturally, he swept the cash back into its bag, then dialed 911.

At Bellevue Hospital Princess' stomach was pumped and she was revived.

In the waiting room, Zest paced. Couldn't wait to see her, to find out why his money had been removed from his stash. Why she was trying to end her life. Good thing he wasn't alone, because he may've lost his mind trying to make sense of something that made no sense. He watched Bones and Capri interact, wishing he could call on them for advice, tell them what they didn't know, what they didn't need to know. While he was deep in thought, Capri stepped to him and said, "We out. Hit me on the hip when you find out something."

A little misty in the eyes Bones said, "Let my sista know I was here. And that I love her."

Zest nodded, was about to find out how long it would be before he could see Princess when Capri grabbed his arm and said, "You know we still got work to do, right?"

"Would you want me saying something like that to you if it were your girl?"

"That product will be here tomorrow, and we need you focused."

Zest yanked his arm from Capri's grasp, said, "Nothing is sacred, is it?"

Slouched back in his Benz wagon, Bones was now aware of

the reason Princess didn't show at Sylvia's a couple days ago. And why she never returned his calls. And it disturbed him. She was one of the few remaining family members he had, someone he adored deeply and planned to have around for a long time to come.

Capri slid into the passenger seat, and said, "Shoot Uptown to Spanish Harlem," with not an inkling of concern for Princess in his voice. "Then take me to the garage to get my car."

Bones lit up a stoge, then pulled off shaking his head. Capri leaned back, made a phone call and asked for Katrina. He wanted to see where her head was, and as he expected, Katrina said, "We can't wait to see you again."

Out the side of his eye, Bones glared wondering what Capri was up to. He knew exactly who Katrina was. Listening intently, he heard Capri say, "Tell me you want me."

"I want you," she returned.

"Tell me you need me."

"I need you."

Bones tuned in until he was distracted by the traffic tightening around 98th Street. Knowing Manhattan like the back of his hand, he was able to maneuver around the gridlock. But he couldn't avoid what was up ahead.

A checkpoint.

And then, "Pri, you gotta get behind the wheel. No license."

Bones threw it in park, Capri hung up, and swiftly they switched seats. As soon as Capri moved back into drive, they were approached by a boy in blue with the youthful look of a rookie.

His blue eyes all over them, he said, "License, registration, and insurance card."

Handing over everything, Capri asked, "What's going on out here?"

Upon checking the requested credentials, the cop said, "We have three dead on the corner of 106th and Lexington."

"Three dead, huh?"

"I'm asking the friggin' questions! Now, why are you driving Princess Quinnones' car?"

"Because the law doesn't say I can't, unless I'm unlicensed."

On that note the cop walked off, saying, "I'll be right back.'

Once the view was clear, Capri said, "That look like Nickels' truck."

Bones said, "Look real messy over there."

"The white Volvo. I know that car," Capri returned, watching the cop who'd stopped them double back.

"Step out of the vehicle!" he commanded, reinforcement by his side and behind him. "We'd like to search the vehicle."

They now had a better view, having agreed to the search. As they were being patted down for weapons, Capri could see the bodies outlined in chalk. Whoever it was, the residents of Spanish Harlem weren't taking it lightly. They had come out in droves, and two women in particular, both voluptuous, were throwing a fit, wailing their hearts out, fighting to get to one of the bodies. From the sidewalks and windowsills, other watching the search accused the police of brutality and racial profiling. And because it was after dark, it took the police a little longer to say, "It's clean, yous can go."

Barely touching the gas, Capri cruised by 106th and Lexington, his eyes on all the hysteria. While fastening his seatbelt, a reality he didn't want to face was sinking in. The two mamis throwing the fit were none other than the mother of Nickels' children, crying their hearts out.

Just a few hours later, as he sat at a bar throwing shots back, Stink walked up with three cats. One he knew as 730, another he knew as Man-Man, and the other he didn't, but had seen around. Dope boy fresh type cat. Baggie jeans, Uptown Nikes, hat to the back, with a mouth full of gold. Not far from a drunken stupor, Capri said, "What's poppin, Blood?!"

Stink replied, "You know the homie Man and 730…"

Man-Man sent some gang signs at Capri, this real sneaky glare in his eyes, as 730 said, "This my pup, Spaz."

Capri hopped down off his barstool, glared down upon this Spaz kid, said, "Keep banging!"

"Pri, lighten up. Lil homie got some news you can use," Stink whispered into Capri's ear than took a step back.

Adjusting his eyes to the brightness of the lighting behind them, Capri nodded, and the kid said, "Peace, Blood."

Again Capri nodded.

The kid went on to say, "I was on 106th and Lex earlier when this white Volvo pulled up. We was out there G-mackin' and shit. Nickels was saying how when y'all get back it was gonna be like the 80s again. He was talking about hitting me with some work to take to York."

"Shorten that shit, gimme the edited version bee!" Capri ordered.

"Mumbles and Zac did him. Pulled up on some Frank White shit, shot him in the face."

Capri released this exasperated sign before cringing and nearly pulling his curls from his head, deep down knowing had he been handled his business, Nickels would still be amongst the living. "It was two more bodies out there—"

"Zac and Mumbles," the young kid spat out.

"...so he took them bird ass niggas with him?" quizzed Capri, his spirits quickly rising.

"Nah." The kid shook his head. "It was another cat with them. Older cat, wild stocky, dark beard, swat cap real low. Looked real serious."

"Brother Joe!"

"After the boggied Nicks, that cat hit both of them in the back of the head then walked off. They never saw it coming."

"Brother Joe?!"

"Brother Joe."

FOURTEEN

"**M**cCants, what the fuck is going on out there?" Jackson, the supervising agent, queried, his tone rather harsh. "Atkins, you're not exempt!"

Agent Atkins took in a little too much air, then turned to Trent McCants. That was the problem, he was beginning to think. Because of Trent, they weren't moving fast enough.

Jackson spoke again. "What the fuck is going on out there? I'm hearing it from my superiors! Three more dead last night! A total of six, and now the mayor wants to hold a press conference."

"We're making progress," slipped from Trent's arid mouth.

"Shut up, just shut up!" the ranking agent squeezed through his tight lips, glaring out his designer specs at both men. When neither man shoed any emotion, Agent Jackson rose from his leather upholstered chair and marched from behind his cluttered desk. The man's biceps, traps, and pectoral muscles were bulging from the button up shirt that appeared to be constricting his diesel frame. His thighs were practically busting the seams of his tan slacks, his belt gripping his small waist. It was evident he spent many hours in the gym, and didn't need the handgun in his shoulder holster. Standing at six-feet-plus, he peered down on his subordinated and seethed, "The murders are reaching epidemic proportions. I need to know what the fuck is going on out there. My goddamn credentials are being questioned. And I know neither one of you shit-heads want to make my shit list.

No do we?"

Both men knew Jackson had aspirations of one day having his own office in One Federal Plaza, and eventually ruling over the FBI like the legendary crime fighter and chronicled racist J. Edgar Hoover. But Trent could take no more. "I've been with the bureau just as long as you have! So you address me with the same respect I give you! I got a goddamn daughter in her twenties! Be damn if I let you belittle me!"

"You finished McCants?"

"Yeah!"

Eyeing Trent McCants down, Jackson went on to say, "Had it not been for ne you'd be down in Arlington at some training camp doing – nothing! I hand picked you, because I knew you were from the city. Because you have a family here."

"Jackson, I know you expected a photo chart with dozens of photos pinpointing the problem by now, but this one isn't that easy."

"The Midnight Express Diner; do you know that they victim in that slaying lost his mother and a brother in that triple murder on Undercliff Avenue in the Bronx just a few months ago?" Jackson asked like he was a prosecutor on direct. "I connected those dots from this tiny office so there's no reason you shouldn't be making progress.

Agent Atkins thought about the missing tape, wondered what was on it, and how helpful it would've been to have got a hold of it. Pondered briefly, empathizing with his supervisor.

Trent said, "When you got me assigned to this unit I vowed to give it my all. And we're onto some of the majors players out there. And within the next week or two specified targets will be in custody."

"McCants, there's a war going on within that organization. We were on to The Voice and his extortion crew long before I brought you in. I want something new. Something convincing! Something that will stick. And I want the bleeding to stop. Oh, and you don't have a week, you have days."

He walked both agents to his office door and extended his arm as to say, "Get the fuck out!" They took a few steps into the hallway and the door slammed behind them.

"That comic book looking motherfucker got his head way up his ass!"

"He has his reasons," Trent returned as he readjusted the straps on his ballistics vest.

Atkins laughed. "What the hell does that mean??? Are you willing to admit we could have been had this case sewn up, but that you're hindering progress?"

The only way to shake that off was by returning laughter. "You're kidding right, kid?" Trent guipped as a dangerous reality began settling in. "You were there last week, Lady Luck's on their side. We had 'em, but the tape recorder was off."

Atkins was much younger than Trent, but he wasn't slow. "The Black Hummer, Trent. Who was that in the Black Hummer?"

This usually nonchalant and easygoing twenty something agent was now like a terrier barking up Trent's leg. When Trent failed to answer in a timely fashion, he said, "I ran the plates."

"And what came back?" Trent wanted to know.

"Nothing. How odd is that?"

Trent continued down the stairs towards the ground floor and out onto 135th Street where he was greeted by the sun. just a few feet behind, Agent Atkins said, "The scar on the right side of his face, the pain in those eyes; I saw it a couple weeks ago at your home."

Trent spun around. "What?"

"The gut who sat eating apple pie at the Midnight Express Diner. He was driving the Hummer. He dropped your daughter off. You two spoke briefly before he sped off. He was at your home, right?"

Trent slid into their unmarked car, and as he was veering into traffic Atkins said, "Trent, are you dirty?"

At the light, with his foot on the breaks, Trent took to clapping, said, "Yeah, I'm taking money. But I run around with you all times of the night inhaling death and gun smoke so my cover doesn't get blown." After pausing for a few to let his words sink in, Trent whispered, "My personal life and my work are two separate entities, remember that. And the next time you make such an accusation, you better have something to substantiate it."

"Your tight," Atkins returned as the cars behind them began honking their horns. "I apologize."

Mashing the gas, Trent pulled off wondering where Capri was. And if he could've saw the man at the very moment, he may've tried choking him out.

At that very moment Capri was in Trent's Yonkers home putting things in perspective in light of Nickels murder and Princess' suicide attempt. Death was around the corner, a realization Capri was beginning to come to grips with. Bottom line, the streets were finally taking their toll on him.

Patience sat at one end of the sofa, Capri at the other, she planning to visit Princess in the hospital, he recalling their many good times. That day she was looking real mean, yet she was the most beautiful he'd ever seen her. Juxtaposed to any other female in his world, hand down Patience stood alone. And at that very moment, she was all he really wanted.

Just as she took her eyes off him, he reached in his pocket.

"Patience, come here."

"No."

"Girl, stop playing and come here."

"Why?" she said sounding all stank and staring him down. "And for what?"

"Because I said so."

"No, I am not feeling you right about now."

"Why?"

That deep sigh women release when they really want to bust a man's head wide open rushed from her nostrils and mouth.

123

"Capri, nothing hurts more than when we're not clicking. I know there no perfect relationship, but I think what we share is unique and nobody should be able to fuck that up. However, that's not the case. I know there's another woman."

"How you know that?"

"You love sex, and we haven't been together in weeks. You haven't palmed my ass, haven't pressed your mouth against the nape of my neck, and you know how hot that gets me. You haven't told me how pretty my titties are since you came home. No kisses, no calls."

"Women can get insecure. We need validation, affection, attention. We need to know that our man wants us. That he needs us!"

"Come ere," he insisted. When she didn't budge, she slid towards her, leaned in. "I got something for you," he revealed, his hand gradually slipping from his pocket.

"Capri, earrings can't fix this. Not this time."

"What about this?"

Patience's eyes widened in awe. Simultaneously, her frown turned downside up. Then suddenly this inspired feeling overcame her. Before she knew it, she was so close to Capri she could hear the thump of his heart, and the rapidity of its movement mirroring hers. Hand trembling, she took the little black velvet box from Capri's hand, removed the content. Capri took the ring from her grasp, and in the gentlest tone, still macho though, he said, "I had a lot of time to think about this, and with all that's going on I thought now would be the best time to tell you...I want you to be wifey."

Overwhelmed with joy, her whiteness came out and Patience shouted, "Mom, I'm getting married!"

Mrs. Mary, eating from her cup of yogurt, appeared out of nowhere with this smirk on her face. She wasn't sure she heard her daughter correctly. But once she saw the sparkling white ice beautifying the platinum band Capri was holding, Mrs. Mary grinned deeply. He wasn't exactly the type of cat she coveted.

She knew he was a gang banger with the merest provocation. That he was unreliable. And yet, she was moved. How long this would last, she could not predict. But the look on her daughter's face was priceless. And she would relinquish almost anything for that.

Without saying a word, she dashed for her office and returned with a camera bombarding them with flashing light.

Capri slipped the ring onto Patience's ring finger, and it fit perfectly. That was caught on camera as well. All three of them then sat and talked for a while like old times, Mrs. Mary wanting to know how long they'd be engaged, how long before they'd pursue their marriage license, when and where the actual wedding would take place, seeing this as the potential beginning of his upside. There were no definitive answers to any of the questions. Just googly eyes on Patience's behalf, and "I don't know's" from Capri. All were smiling and basking in the moment. And then, Mrs. Mary said, "Well at least, now y'all can start making me some grandbabies. Think y'all ready to be parents? I know I want some grandchildren."

That proverbial lump formed in Capri's throat. And he wondered how much longer he could keep Christine's pregnancy a secret. While he was deep in thought, Patience said, "Yes we are!"

Mrs. Mary said, "Capri, you need to get Trent's blessing too, baby. Ask for his daughter's hand in marriage. You know that, right?"

Capri nodded, but that wasn't on his "to do" list. Far from it.

"I gotta call Tameko!" Patience chimed sashaying off.

Mrs. Mary said, "And you gotta call your father!"

While they were spreading the news, Capri decided to get on the phone too and start cleaning up the mess he had made. He knew he would miss those dick sucks, but less was beginning to feel like more to him.

Looking over his shoulder, he crept out the back door and dialed Asia's number. As the phone rang he thought of words that would let her down easy. Something that wouldn't sting, but would leave no room for misinterpretation.

Answering machine.

At the beep, Capri said, "…Ayyo, this Pri. More or less, I'm calling to say it was fun, you give the best head I ever had, but I need you to lose my number. Don't call me no more. Consider the furniture a severance gift."

He spent the next few minutes hoping she didn't call him back while he was out back on the sun porch or anywhere on the confines of Patience's home for that matter. While doing that he wondered what he was going to do about Christine. Surely she didn't deserve to be cut off. It wasn't her fault he splashed in her. That she was ovulating that night he twisted her out in back of the movie theater. Against his will he became aroused just thinking about the curvacious chocolate bunny carrying his child.

Unbeknownst to him, Patience was creeping up and feeling like she had struck the lotto. She saw the bulge in his sweats, and thinking she was the cause commenced to so something that she'd purposefully withheld from him for far too long. With her mother on the top floor, Patience reached into Capri's sweats and quickly took him into her hungry mouth, pretending his penis was the banana Tameko had her use while teaching her how to give head as they watched a porno in 3-D intently. Almost immediately she was turned on. By the power she now had over him, the writhe of his body, the lustful breathing, the groans of passion coming from deep down in the pit of his stomach as he thrusted himself in and out of her mouth. For a second she felt like Heather Hunter, going at it with reckless abandon. Her mouth was wet, luscious and affective for a first timer. I can do this, she thought. And in little to no time his hot load was in the back of her throat.

She'd finished and was nestled up next to Capri just as the nearing sound of her mother's voice resounded on the other side of the door. Still awestruck and feeling the effects of his climax,

Capri heard Mrs. Mary say, "Your father isn't picking up his phone!"

Agent McCants was conducting some good old surveillance when his phone first began to ring. Atkins had a great view through his night-vision binoculars of a cherry red Tahoe parking alongside a black sedan they tailed to the Bronx undetected. Deep in the cut behind the 149th Street Aamco Car Wash and Gas Station, Brother Joe slid out the dark sedan and then a young kid hopped down out the red Chevy truck. They shook hands before Brother Joe handed off a small duffel bag. Atkins zoned in a little more wishing he could hear what was being said...

"There's fifteen grand in the bag."

"Where's the rest?" the kid asked a little too confident for Brother Joe's liking.

"You get the rest when I start seeing some progress."

"What you mean?"

Glaring down on the five-foot-three twerp, Brother Joe removed the gold toothpick from his mouth, said, "Capri and Stink. How can I get close to them? In the last month, they've become invisible."

"That wasn't part of the agreement. You said you just wanted to know if and when y'all would be under attack again."

"Well a lots changed since then."

"Like what?"

"They left three of ours dead, and my man with almost a half mil in property damages. And as of lately, they've become untouchable."

"I don't know what this is over, I just told you what I do know."

"Just listen," Brother Joe began as he waved over two men in the sedan to join them. "I want you to show these two cats how to maneuver around these parts we call home."

A tall slender cat and a short brolic fellow hastily approached. The tall one was rocking tan khakis, a flannel and some navy Chucks, looking like Snoop Dogg. His partner was sporting a dark blue Dickie suit and blue Cons, cornrows hanging way down his back.

"Ayyo, you brought some Crip niggas to Harlem???"

"I don't' know, the only color I know is green. And the only people I ride for are dead presidents. You better get hip, youngster! Now y'all introduce ya'selves."

"Baby Blue!" spat the short one.

"Loc E Loc. Hoover Street Crips," the lanky cat relayed in a mud-thick west coast accent.

"Killa Blood! 115thsStreet. I don't shake hands." With that, Loc's hand was left afloat. "Brother Joe, this ain't right."

"Trent, answer that goddamn phone so I can concentrate! It's been ringing and ringing nonstop!"

Trent was snapping away, getting it all on film, his phone wailing away like a baby in a shitty diaper. When he finally did pick up, Mrs. Mary said, "What took you so long to answer your phone?!"

"Why? What's wrong, baby?"

"Our little girl's getting married!"

The camera slipped from Trent's grasps. "You serious?"

"Capri got a ring and everything!"

"That sonofabitch is dead smack in the middle of this investigation, and he's..."

"Trent, keep it down! Something's going on!" Atkins warned with his eyes on the prize, an avenue of his supervisor's shit-list.

"...in my..."

"Trent, what are you talking about?" Mrs. Mary queried noticing that his usually debonair voice was jacked by that of a grouch.

Trent whispered, "People are dying out here, and he may be right in the middle of it."

"I cannot hear you, Trent," Mrs. Mary chided.

"I said, I'm against it!"

"Really?"

"Really!"

"When you thought he was gonna enter the draft and you were trying to get him to sign with your sports agent friend, he was your future son-in-law. But when things went sour, you –"

"Is she pregnant?"

"Mo! They're in love."

"That's bullshit!" Trent stammered, his green eyes nearly snake-like slits.

"Man, there comes a time when we must all become our own man. Broaden our horizons. See past color. The world we live in today isn't ran by color, it's ran by status. I got a vision, an right now you fuckin' with my shit."

Brother Joes was a success at concealing his true intentions and pushing forward a fantasy to obtain any means of leverage. He knew Action was on his last leg and it was time to play for the future. His future. With his hand extended for the trader's, he said, "I'm make you a boss. Fuck answering to Stink."

Man-Man looked pass the crispy fatigue suit, Beef-n-Broccoli Timbs, right at Brother Joe's hand. He could tell the man had experience a lot. Far more than all the talk in the streets. Two of his fingers were jammed, his knuckles were scarred up with teeth marks, and his nails through clean had a dingy look about them. He thought of all the quick cash Stink would be stacking off that move he made with Capri and Zest, and his envy quickly turned to jealousy. "What you need me to do?" he asked, his hand now in the monster grip of Brother Joe.

Angered, Trent was back to snapping away. It was the breakthrough they needed. He had a possible payoff, two different crews shaking hands, faces and license plates. And then - a picture of the man holding the duffel pulling a wad from the bag just before boarding the Chevy truck.

Brother Joe and the Crips pulled off as Trent said, "Follow the money!"

The sedan pulled into the gas station and the Tahoe swerved

out onto 149th Street. Agent Atkins let a few cars go ahead of them then began the tail. They followed the Tahoe into Harlem. To the Juice Bar on 145th Street. A liquor store on Lenox Avenue. And eventually to 134th Street and 8th Ave where he played host to a bunch of chicks in tight jeans and heels, with long hair and long nails.

"What now?" quizzed Atkins.

"I don't know. Thought he would lead us to a stash house. A upper tier player."

"We should've followed Abraham! Damn!"

They should have.

Just as Atkins made that statement, Brother Joe and the cats he had imported from South Central to shake things up on the East Coast were entering an upscale eatery on Queens Blvd. Brother Joe told the sexy hostess he was there meeting Anwar Outen and was swiftly escorted to a table where the crime czar was seated with his daughter. Immediately Brother Joe noticed her pupils were dilated, and her usually confident aura wasn't as alarming. However, she was still succulent, tits sitting up high and kissing. Had she not been his man's daughter, Lord only knows how fast he'da tried to enact his scandalous thoughts. But he managed to keep his eyes out her cleavage, and his mind on convincing Action that they would be much more constituted without now that Zac and Mumbles were goners, though he would never admit to picking them off himself.

Action whispered something to the young beauty that made her roll her eyes, then he and Brother Joe stalked to the bar area, leaving her to entertain. It didn't take her long to pick their brains, and thought it would be a good idea to tell Capri she was sitting at a table with some Crips. Leaving them alone, she grabbed her champagne glass and headed outside. Within minutes she had Capri on the phone. "Trina, what up?"

"On my way uptown to see you," she poked, hoping he'd encourage it.

"Where you at now?"

"With my dad. Him and Brother Joe got these corny ass Crip niggas with them."

"Oh yeah? From where, Bed Stuy?"

"Nah, Cali homie. And they look crazy."

"How many?"

"Just two. Loc and Baby Blue. Said they're here on serious business," she revealed, then said, "I wanna see you."

Taking advantage of her passion, he said, "It's nine now, meet me at M&G's at ten. See what else you can find out before you boogie."

"I'll be there."

"You didn't tell your pops about us, did you?"

"Hell no!"

"Ai'ight. Ten o'clock."

Katrina shut her c-phone and ambled back to the table. As she approached, Action who was now slouched back, said, "Where were you?"

"Out front on the phone! Why?"

"Because I asked."

She sucked her teeth, said, "How much longer are we gonna be here?"

"Have a seat, we haven't even ordered yet. And we still have a lot to discuss. This whole taking off from school, I don't like it."

With one hand rested on her hip and the other griping the champagne glass, she replied, "I'm not even hungry. I'll grab something later, or eat at Iris'. I'm spending the night over there. And we can talk tomorrow."

"Katrina."

"I'ma just grab a burger or something."

"Have a seat, they'll be leaving shortly."

Katrina strutted pass Loc E. Loc towards her seat, but she didn't sit, she grabbed her Fendi bag and said, "I'm not staying."

131

Action was appalled. He knew Katrina was under the influence of some outside interference, that somebody was in her ear, possibly her panties as well, and felt it necessary to maintain control. "Sit down…now," he seethed, noticing the shock in Brother Joe's eyes, the result of Katrina's disobedience. "I'm not done talking to you."

Katrina said, "I'll call you later, if it's that important," then started towards the door.

Action had never saw her so defiant, so disrespectful. No one had.

"Joe, I'll be right back."

Outside in the parking lot Action and Katrina engaged in a blistering joust of words. Cars were pulling in and patrons were walking out, as the clouds above rolled and roared through the darkness of the night.

"If you ever disrespect me again like that, you're gonna need a surgeon to readjust you face. Do you hear me?" Action forewarned pulling his daughter out of the spotlight.

"Let me go!" Katrina shouted as she broke free of the grip Action had on her arm. "I'm grown daddy. Recognize!"

"You're grown when you get the fuck from under my roof! You're grown when you know what the fuck it takes to make it in this world! You ain't grown because you now know what a wet ass feels like! And until then you're gonna do what the fuck I say."

"Where did that come from?"

"A muthafucka who commands respect!"

Katrina couldn't believe her father had spoken to her like that. And though she was on a coke induced high, she for the first time saw her father through the eyes everyone else did. "I didn't think me wanting to have fun would make you so bitter, so vulgar, make you talk to me like I'm one of your flunkies, Action!"

"You will address me as daddy! Even after I'm long gone."

"A daddy would never question his daughter's growth by

insinuating she getting her ass wet. What, are you jealous?
"Of what?" Action laughed so coldly. "Are you serious?"
"That's how you're acting. Makes me think you wanna fuck me!"

Action slapped her so hard, traces of her lipstick were left behind in his palm. Her head jerked back and snapped forward in slow motion. The champagne glass slipped from her grasp, smacking the concrete and splashing all over their shoes. Simultaneously, her purse hit the ground. It was the first time he'd ever laid a hand on her.

"Now take to' ass home!"

For a moment Katrina had absolutely no idea where she was. Mouth agape and in shock, she knelt for her purse. While squatting, her left heel came from beneath her. Seeing that ankle turn brought back that fatherly instinct. Action grabbed her wrist in an attempt to help her, and she shouted, "Get the fuck off me!"

"I'm try'na help you!"

He let her go and she staggered over to her car, got in, and locked the doors. She let her visor down to check the damages, and a photo of her, Iris and Capri taken on South Beach fell into her lap. She glared into the mirror to notice her lips were a bit swollen. There was also a whelp on her left check the length of Action's huge mitts. To say she was humiliated would've robber her of emotion.

After a few minutes of pampering, she looked down at the photo. It was at that moment she no longer saw her father as her pillar of strength.

She put her key in the ignition, turned the stereo on. She then slid her shades over her eyes and made moves. When her car wheeled wildly out onto the streets, all Action could do was pray she didn't become prey. He had enough problems on his hands.

About twenty minutes later the skies began to cry. Action would periodically peak out the window beside him as he explained exactly what was expected, how he wanted this gang war to begin and end, and exactly what was at stake.

Brother Joe listened intently, thinking that if this was pulled off, that if these skilled bangers, the arch rivals of their troublesome problem, were able to fill the void they lacked in, he could go back to money bag stashing, playing daddy to his step kids, and stop living in worry of possibly being next on Capri's hit list. Prior to the insurgence of the Blood gang, the city had never experienced a movement of such magnitude, with such structure, so many of the worse niggas playing for the same team. They were feeling the effects of it.

And in the heart of the city, Action's daughter was trying to explain to Capri what happened, instead of what she could find out. He sat in the hallway of his old building in Drew Hamilton projects, arms folded across his chest, looking on with no pity. It was in that very building that his mother was killed at the hands of her father.

In a carefree tone he said, "Are you done bitching?"

"What you mean?"

"It ain't the end of the world. A little more coke, you'll forget the whole thing."

"Fuck you," she said never in a million years expecting to be smacked twice in the same night. But that's what her mouth had gotten her. Only this one didn't send her off in a rage, it made her hotter for Capri.

After consoling her then finding her some powder, he took her to Zest and Princess' old Lenox Terrace apartment. One step into the flat and they both could hear the erotic moaning of a woman. It turned Katrina on. Made Capri mad curious. As he neared the master bed, the sounds of sex got louder. When he got to the bedroom door, he noticed Bones in raw form, sine big booty broad with red hair and skin taking the dick like a champ. Katrina got a glimpse and reached for Capri's dick, only to be halted in process.

"I wanna ride. Want you to make me feel good. Wanna taste

you. Feel you cumming."

"Not now," Capri told her.

"Why?" she wanted to know, again reaching for his crotch.

"Because I said so."

Shortly after they took seats in the living room, the sounds of sex subsided. Then appeared Bones with his puny chest out, tightening the belt on his jeans with a smirk on his face, and obviously not expecting more company.

Capri pulled him to the side and said, "Yo, I'm going to check Christine before I go back to Yonkers. Katrina's gonna stay the night, get her mind right. Ai'ight?"

"Her pops know—"

"Nah, just keep her company til I get back."

Bones looked on confused, but said, "Ai'ight. Let me run downstairs to the store real quick, get some food, blunts and more condoms."

"Go 'head, and hurry up."

Bones grabbed his shirt and jacket, his gun and keys. On his way downstairs, he shook his head wondering what Capri was up to. Fucking with a nigga's daughter was a no-no. especially Action's. when he exited the building lobby, there was still a light drizzle falling. But the desire to check on his platinum Benz wagon sitting on them matching BBSs was irresistible. And that would be the very reason he didn't peep the Ford Explorer pull up on 135th. Or the doors swing open. When he finally realized what was going down, it was too late. After being pistol whipped unconscious by a kid with a cut on his face, then flung into the truck like a rag doll by another cat with LAVA tattooed across the right side of his neck, he was sped off into the night.

FIFTEEN

"**A** thank you would be nice."

"For what???"

"I gotta say it?"

"Your daughter should be thanking you. Ain't nothing wrong with them clothes hanging in her closet anyway."

"Dom' can't wear them clothes in her closet!"

"He had something new to wear for the first few days of the new school year. You didn't have to—"

"What about the movies?" Nitti grinned.

"We appreciate."

Nitti was feeling real good about himself, and his future. He had a sharp Caesar, waves spinning, crisp gear, and an upcoming meeting with a couple goons from his hood. Since being back in the good graces of his baby mama was the icing on his cake. Since he'd been home from prison she'd been making him feel entitled to ecstasy. Two, three times a day she would reach in his jeans, make him achieve size and girth, then give him that empowering leer, the one that screamed pleasure. Her mouth would be watering, and then in seconds touching the dome of his penis, lubricating and prepping him for the supreme blow job. Like clockwork his hand would go to her braids, and he'd move his rod in and out, nice and slow.

He touched himself just thinking about what would pop off once the kids were fed and fast asleep. Caressed wondering where his baby mama had disappeared to, then wandered through the cabinets looking for saucers to put the kids' Chinese food on. With the kids finally situated at the table, and a lustful prelude in mind, he went searching for her long legs that fat ass and them plump tits, his mouth now watering. As he neared her bedroom – grinning and aroused – a familiar voice jarred him.

"...More or less, I'm calling to say it was fun, you gave me the best head I ever had, but I need you to lose my number. Don't call me no more. Consider the furniture a severance gift."

Nitti's eyes filled with rage, as his legs nearly gave out. Paralyzed with paranoia, he stood watching as she hit the replay feature then put her head down. "Daffany!" he shouted.

Startled, she spun around on her four inch heels, and he said, "What's really good with you?"

"Excuse me?"

"Of all the dicks you suck; my man!?"

"That ain't your fucking man!" she so boldly stated, her hip poked out in arrogance. "And don't be questioning me about my business in my apartment!"

"That's Capri Hayward on the fucking answering machine! Daff, I know his voice! I did two bids with him! And you had him in here! His dick in your mouth for some fucking furniture?!"

"Daddy, what's wrong?" their daughter quizzed looking up at them.

"Nothing, babygirl. Go finish eating ya food."

As soon as the young child walked off, Nitti said, "Of all the niggas in the city – him?" He walked in a tight circle, fist balled up. "Sexing him while I masturbate."

"Mommy, what's masturbate?" the little girl asked.

"Get your ass back to that table before I beat it!" she shouted, scaring her daughter half to death. She then glared at Nitti like he was a roach on the stovetop. "When you went to jail, were we together?"

"Nah, no, but--?"

"Then ain't nobody try'na hear that shit. Matter fact, you

can get the fuck up out of here since you got a problem with how I choose to pass my time."

"...Consider the furniture a severance gift."

That was enough to make Nitti roll out. Slam the door behind him. Take the steps downstairs. Find himself traveling west towards University Avenue on foot, a 22-oz. Heine in hand, looking for someone to vent to.

When he got to 174th and University he peeped Lava posted up smoking a blunt alone. Some other neighborhood cats taking up space. Then Dave's GTI sitting by the projects. On the other side of the street, a black 540i BMW caught his eye. Tackhead was leaned back on it, the girl whose name he didn't know talking to him louder than need br.

"I said I wanted him fucked up, not trunked!" Nitti heard the red bone express. "What are you gonna do to him?"

And then Tackhead said, "Haven't decided yet, but I'll let you know when I do," in a slick slur.

Tyanna was sick, betrayal suffusing every fiber of her being. She hadn't seen her crew in weeks. Hadn't been home either. And barely looked herself in the mirror. Too busy trying to have her sister's murder avenged, and Bones dealt with for smacking her – paying handsomely with the prize between her legs.

"You shoulda did Capri like that," she stammered, tugging at the sleeve of the big fella's Coogi sweater. "I just wanted him fucked up."

It was obvious she still had feelings for Bones. That wasn't sitting well with Tackhead, and he quickly became filled with jealously. Confidence is king, and at that moment he was lacking it. Eyes half mast, he chugged down a little of his champagne, turned to his contractors and said, "The boiler room."

Scarface Dave was a leader in his own rite, capable of starting his own gang, and loved his independence and allegiance to no one. but he was paid nicely for his services, so he waved Lava over and did as he was told. Did it with a smile on his face too.

Bones' face was covered in blood, and he was oblivious to his surroundings when he was dragged from the Explorer. But then he recognized Tyanna standing beneath a street sign reading MONTGOMERY Ave. and then he noticed Tackhead, a heavy weight he'd seen around. That's when reality hit. This was retribution. "You got me set up, bitch?"

Glaring pass the blood, the bumps and bruises, Tyanna saw his face and immediately sulked. But, there was nothing she could do. The damage was done. The moment Tyanna told Tackhead about her drama back in Harlem. Like most portly players, Tackhead wasn't exactly a favorite amongst the females, and had to go that extra mile to maintain enthusiasm whenever it arised. But murder wasn't on the menu. Until now. With Bones out the way, Tyanna would be all his.

Ina swift motion, Tyanna advanced towards Bones with compassion in her eyes, only to have Tackhead snatch her up and wrap her in his arms. "The boiler room, Dave. Now."

Tyanna watched in agony, Tackhead holding her tightly. As they hauled Bones into the alleyway leading to the basement of the building, his phone fell from his waist. There weren't many people paying attention that night, so Tyanna and some base-head Rican chick were the only two to notice it.

Minutes later Dave and Lava emerged from the six story tenement without their captor. They'd stomped him out, relieved him of his jewels, car keys, gun and left him behind tied to a chair, gasping for air. Since his uncle was the super, Tack wasn't worried about anyone finding him.

"I'm going back for the Benz!" Scarface Dave spat, noticing Nitti was early for their little meeting and just a few feet from them.

"Leave the car where it be," Tack forewarned, aware removing it would only boil suspicion.

"That shit got BBS and TVs. I need that," Dave replied, lighting a stoge. "Franco! Come on, take this ride with me!"

"It's Nitti! How many times I gotta tell you that, Dave?"

"Franc Nitti was an enforcer. Get your weight up, and I'll think about addressing you as such," Dave replied watching Tackhead carry Tyanna off. As soon as he was out of earshot, Dave said, "I'm going to get that car! Fuck what that fat mufucka talking about."

That he did,

While Scarface Dave was cruising across the bridge, Nitti said, "I heard that chick say something about some kid named Capri."

"Yeah. Tank put some paper on his head for her. Money supposedly had her sister plucked.

There was a pause, and them, "That nigga was fucking my babymoms, bee."

"Nah!"

"Word da mutha."

Dave glanced over at Nitti and busted out laughing. "Everybody done had a slice of that ass. Them kids from 175th and Macombs Road. A couple of them Jamaicans from 174th and Davidson. Them Blood kids from 183rd."

"Fuck out of here, nigga!"

"And word is the head game is retarded."

"Stop playing, sun."

"Dead ass, bee. She ain't cheap either, from what I hear."

Nitti didn't say another word, just sat silent. Didn't speak until they were pulling alongside the Benz wagon. He said, "I still love her."

Dave didn't respond, just said, "Drive my car back to the Bronx."

"Yo, how that nigga het a name like...Tackhead?"

"Look at that ugly mafucka's little ass head!"

SIXTEEN

Another night in Harlem was overtaken by daylight. Capri couldn't recall falling asleep, but recognized that he was well rested when his eyes popped open, surrendering with a squint to the undesired sunlight coming through the venetian blinds. He stretched then checked his wrist for the time. It was almost six A.M. and again he'd broken his promise to Patience. He released a gust of air imagining what she was thinking, then took a peek at Katrina who lay motionless on his chest. Her face didn't look as bad as it did the night before, but it was still swollen. He couldn't help but inhale the goodness of her hair before slipping from beneath her. As he rose to his feet, out came, "Bones! Why the fuck you ain't wake me up when you came back?"

No response.

"Bones, I know you hear me nigga!"

The red bone appeared massaging her scalp. And in the sunlight Capri immediately recognized her from a few music videos. As he sized her up, she said, "He hasn't come back yet."

"Word?"

"Word. I thought he'd be back by the time I got out the shower, but—"

"He never came back?"

In the corner of the girl's eye was Katrina as she told Capri, "Nope. Want me to call him?"

"Yeah. Call him, see what up, where the fuck he at. This

ain't like him to leave me hanging."

"What about me? Do I look like a chick you leave hanging?"

"Nah. Call him, see what's really good."

In a flirty gesture she put her hand out.

"What?"

"Your phone," she said with her mouth looking real pouty and cute.

Capri was used to women being sweet on him. And he knew their language, but he wasn't trying to hear it at the moment. Katrina said, "You want his phone or an autograph?"

She rolled her green eyes and Katrina then dialed Bones. Demonstrated her sexiness while waiting for an answer. Bones wasn't her dude – in fact they'd just met a week prior to that day at a video shoot – but a pang of jealousy jilted her when she heard feminine yawns on the other end.

"Who dis?" she quizzed sharply.

Capri reached for the phone with some choice words at the tip of his tongue. But green eyes pushed it away, again asking, "Who is this?"

When the person breathing on the other end of the phone said nothing, girlie tossed Capri the phone and said, "I'm out of here! I ain't got no time for this. Niggas try'na hit this all the way from the South Bronx to Jamaica Queens!"

"Put Bones on the phone," said Capri, watching girlie saunter off. And with so much hostility, contempt, arrogance and anger, "I know this ain't Capri?" she shouted into his ear.

"Who this?"

"The bitch who got your man trunked last night. The bitch that's gonna do everything in her power to make sure you pay for killing her sister! That's who!"

Capri was stuck. Being accused of murder by the police was one thing, but a murder victim's sibling was another. As if his plate wasn't already cluttered. He grabbed a fistful of his curly crown and pulled wishing it were Tyanna's tongue. The look on his grill made Katrina nervous, and the green eyed red boned vixen slow her stroll. He paced for a few seconds oblivious of their eyes, thinking of his comrade and his safety. While dong so he paged him, then asked, "So what up, why Bones?"

Tyanna reaffirmed her position, further stating, "Enjoy your last days. You got a date with death, buster." Then hung up.

Capri found himself pacing again, before telling both girls they had to roll.

Katrina said, "Pri, where you going?"

"can't tell you that. Cal me later!"

Christine had began showing. Not just in the stomach, but in the breasts too. Her nose had even widened, and her face was filling out. Yet, Capri still found her extremely attractive and in the most convincing of tones, said, "You look good," when he got to her apartment.

"Thank you," she gushed happy to be in his presence, though she could tell something was different. She tried making eye contact, warming him up to her touch, before saying, "What up, boo? Talk to me."

The night before he decided to tell Christine that he'd just gotten engaged, though he knew she wouldn't understand and it would hurt her. That he'd be there for her and their child. and always support her in whatever she chose to do. But in some weird twist of fate, that had all changed. And instead he had gone there to say, "I need you to call Tyanna."

"Why?"

"I think something happened to Bones."

"For slapping her?" she asked, surprise widening her eyes.

"He slapped her?"

Christine thought back the last time she'd seen Tyanna, and how disturbed the girl was about her sister's death. Thought about how bad she felt after going downstairs and finding Bones had spazzed on her. In a slow nod her head moved up and down as she said, "Yeah, a few weeks ago. In front of millions too. Right before we feel out, and right after she found out her sister was dead."

"Why did y'all fall out?"

"Girl stuff," she said too ashamed to give the details.

"Call her."

Lips pursed, and a bit overwhelmed, Christine got Tyanna on the phone. She could hear the soft, calm, but powerful sound of Tyanna breathing. And at that moment she knew something wasn't right. "Tyanna?"

"What do you want?"

"To know how you are? Where you are?"

"Funny you call now after almost a month. Funny you call right after I speak to Capri. Is he there with you? Of course he is! Tell him I meant what I said. He gonna feel what my sis—"

Capri snatched the phone, covered the receiver with his hand. "What'd she say?"

"She knows you're here," Christine whispered concerned. Capri put the phone to his face and started to refuting her allegations, stating, "I was in Miami."

"Fuck does that mean? Niggas is getting niggas rocked from behind the wall. Over the phone."

"Ty, you tripping."

"You tripping!" she snapped. "It was all good in the hood 'til you came home. Lux was alive. Christine was my girl. People wasn't dying! Just remember this, you reap what you sew."

"You fooling! Where's Bones? I paged him and he didn't call back. How'd you get his phone?"

"He won't be smacking nobody else, that's all you need to know."

"Why, what did you do?"

"And oh yeah,...Christine knows about Patience, but um, I wonder how she'd feel if she found out you sticking your dick in that nasty bitch Asia. Haha. That's right...you think she's Daffany. Don't feel bad, even I thought she was Daffany – until I met her baby father last night."

"What are you talking about?"

"Thought that would strike a chord," she cackled.

Talk about being humiliated. Capri's whole swagger took a back seat to that seed of uncertainty. Daffany was Asia. Asia was Daffany.

As he got a grip on himself, he heard a masculine voice that didn't belong to Bones say, "Why you on the phone with li'l mama?"

Yeah, that was Tackhead, his eyes all over that light trail of hair coming up out of Tyanna's jeans leading to her bellybutton. He stopped at the laced bra that hid her luscious tatas from him. Reaching for the clasp in her cleavage, he again asked, "Who you talking to this early?"

Tyanna addressed her caller first, "You're gonna die young, just like my sister did," before concluding the call. She then leered at Tackhead and murmured, "Some people from my past. But you, you are my future."

Through clever seduction she placed him under a mystified spell. To him Tyanna was like a goddess. Normally at that time in the morning he'd be preoccupied with that rush of dope fiends, but she had him sprung. He couldn't even think straight.

Topless. Tyanna crawled atop his mammoth body, slipping her tongue into his ear, whispering, "I wanna have your baby."

It may've seemed romantic and even quaint – just as him giving her $10,000 to forget about what Bones did – but it was all an act. She may've been young and just a bit naïve, but the nubile beauty wasn't cheap. Everything he hustled so hard for was on the verge to becoming charity. When she stripped naked and rejoined him in bed he thought he finally had her heart.

"Like that, don't you?" she quipped, straddling him.

"No question, ma."

"Then you're gonna love this."

She started riding him reverse cowgirl, then took him in her mouth, before eventually pulling her double jointed legs behind her neck and letting him munch, grinning the entire time. He ate her out confessing his adoration, and made her cum determined to prove it.

Around noon he loaded his Suburban up and headed for Harlem. Scarface Dave, Lava, and two of his lieutenants were in the back. Tyanna rode shotgun. At the stoplight on 145th and Eight Avenue Tyanna could see her old block was still thriving without her. She noticed a congregation. Capri, Stink and Zest sticking out like sore thumbs, their spotless cars lining the curbside.

"Listen, my B.M. said she's most likely up in the Bronx with some cat named Tack. And nine times out of ten he had Bones snatched for her."

"Nickels is gone, and now this," Zest said shaking his head.

"Did they ask for some money?" Stink asked.

"Nah. No demands. At least not yet."

Zest thought of Princess and all she'd been through in the last week. Wondered how she'd take this, her little brother being kidnapped. Definitely wouldn't be easy if they didn't get him back. Although they were no longer a couple, a large portion of him sympathized with her.

"So what the fuck is really good?" asked BB a young stud from the Drew Hamilton projects always looking to establish himself as an asset to the Blood Nation. "What we gonna do?"

"I got a homie from those parts by the name of Nitti that can probably put a face with the name Tackhead," Capri replied. "Just gotta catch up with him."

"Fuck that, let's go through there!" Zest suggested. "The more time we waist the less his chances of making it back."

"There's something else," said Capri his hand kneading the scar on his face. "Action done brought some crabs to Harlem…"

Man-Man stood stunned, mouth agape. He couldn't understand how Capri'd gained knowledge of the bangers in blue so fast.

"…but right now, we gotta find out what's up with the lil

homie."

As they politicked, the 'Burban rolled by. For Tyanna it was as though everything was moving in slow motion. She missed home, hated her new arrangements, and there stood the man who'd selfishly changed the landscape of her life. "There he go right there in the red Avirex jacket! And that's his cousin in the black Vanson. Get 'em!" she demanded like a real boss bitch.

"Damn near all them niggas got on red!" someone stammered.

"The light skin one with the curly hair!" she pointed.

"And you ain't tell me they was banging," Tackhead blurtted, his grip tightening on the steering wheel. "And wasn't he a McDonald's All-American some years back? Had a tournament going on over the summer?"

"Yeah," Tyanna returned rolling her eyes. "What they mean?"

"From balling to banging," Tackhead snarled, shaking his head. "What a waste of talent."

He cruised slowly pass 143rd Street, eyes on colorful cast and their luxurious fleet of whips. Quickly, he realized he wasn't dealing with kids and felt a second guess creeping up on him. Both his lieutenants thought they saw a ghost. Head to take a second look. Scarface Dave and Lava remained poised, both ready to open fire and earn their paper. And then suddenly, "Yo, Shaka, that's the nigga who robbed us at Esso back in May! That nigga took my Lex!"

"Thought I'd never see him again," Shaka admitted remembering that night Capri smacked him silly with the .44 auto.

Tackhead was lost. "I thought y'all told me—"

"That nigga took my fucking chain and ring too! Shaka revealed stirring in his seat and sparking a Newport.

"—y'all came out the club and the car was gone?" Tackhead grilled, peaking back over his shoulder at his youngins. "Y'all got jacked and ain't tell me? Y'all niggas lied! Type of shit is

147

y'all on?"

Head down, Fame said, "Too embarrassed. They left us on the Westside Highway buck naked."

By the time everyone had assessed realization of they'd just learned they'd long passed the corner Capri and his cipher were holding down. Lava, a brute fellow in his twenties, reached for the mini mac under his army jacket, said, "Go back through there."

Tackhead busted a U-turn on 135th and Eight Ave, swerving back towards Drew Hamilton thinking of how fast his life had taken a turn. He could feel the air thickening. Hadn't been this hot for him in years. He was so distracted and consumed with what was about to transpire that de didn't even notice the jet black Crown Victoria with the official plates cruise by. But he peeped the second one. the sun wasn't far from zenith so it was very bright out making it nearly impossible for his eyes to penetrate the tinted windows. When he checked the rearview he seen Scarface Dave pulling his weapon too. But Dave had more on his mind than bringing the pain to Capri. He couldn't believe his luck. Thought he'd have to hunt this Capri cat down. As he pulled the lever back, watched the slug enter the chamber, got in the firing position, he decided the cats he was riding with and for were soft, and didn't deserve their stake in the game or the rewards they were reaping from it. Once this job was finished, he planned to clean them out then head for Atlanta where he had some family. Even the glitter on Tyanna's wrist, ears and hand was looking real good.

Only, it wouldn't be that easy.

"Where the fuck they got hat fast?!" Scarface Dave screeched.

SEVENTEEN

Action was beginning to feel like the city no longer belonged to him, that stronghold he once had slowly slipping away. How could this possibly be happening? he wanted to know. His subconscious said, "Nothing lasts forever."

As he peered from the balcony of his 3,500 sq. foot Astoria, Queens's compound, wealth stared back at him. A dark blue 560 Benz, a pearl white suicide-door Continental Lincoln, a black STS Caddy Coupe, a pearl V12 and a platinum Rolls Royce lined his driveway. The fir trees anchoring his manicured lawn reminded him of his upbringings. Was a long ways from small town Tuscaloosa, Alabama where he first realized what aggression and oppression could produce, the country having still been segregated at the time.

Born the summer of 1946 to a half breed waitress in her late teens, he wasn't like most children. His fair skinned mother never offered him suckling, rarely looked his way, and often would disappear for weeks leaving him with her prostitute friends. By the time he was thirteen he barely knew her and the authorities knew him. He'd been accused of slaughtering some farmer's Angus cow and taking off with some prime cut. Accused of stabbing a white supremacist who'd ripped his caretaker off for some pussy. And finally, a suspect in a barnyard arson.

In the sweetest of tones, he recalled some of his caretaker's last words to him being, "If they don't get ya for stabbin' that racist, that farmer's definitely gonna be after your lil tail. And he catch ya, they'll probably try and hang ya up. You gotta get away from here. Gon' now. And don't come back."

"But, I didn't do it," he remembered lying, as well as the lovely scent of her bosom. She had the flair of an entertainer, and the looks to match, but the heart of a subservient menial. So before she could become an enabler to his accusers, he took off. And the only thing that mattered was persevering. That anger and determined nature of his never left him. But by the time he was fifteen this industrious nature was driving his as well. So it wasn't hard to make alliances. And one of them led him from the bayous of Louisiana to the city of bright lights, where dreams come true.

At the time Harlem was still in the renaissance stages, Martin was still marching, the NAACP wasn't advancing fast enough, so he took to the streets where he had no problem making ends meet. Before he knew it the would had lost Martin and Malcolm. While they mourned, he capitalized exerting his will and rising real fast. And by the time the community knew what hit them, it was too late.

Removing him from his reverie was the sight of a car speeding onto his property. When the driver jumped out, he knew death was near.

"My fucking daughter's trying to drive me into an early grave," he thought aloud with his Cuban cigar between his teeth. "Give me a damn heart attack."

Katrina along with Iris, emerged in black motorcycle leathers, dark jeans and boots, with Gucci shades over their eyes. Followed closely by her girl she trooped across the lawn, into the sunlight, towards the main entrance.

Action's cigar fell from his mouth.

"Trina, I still can't believe your dad smacked you for nothing," Iris said, having just heard about it.

"Yeah, me neither," replied Katrina, looking back at the

mess they made cutting through the lawn.

Gaiting from his one place of solace to address the lack of respect, Action was halted in his tracks by his son. At twelve he stood a little under six feet. Everyone knew he was going to be tall like his dad. "What up A.J.? you good, baby boy?"

"Yes. How about you?"

"I seen better days, but hey I ain't complaining," he replied, smiling.

Anwar Outen Jr. was very smart for a 12-year kid. Bit just in the books, but when it came to common sense as well. He knew something was different. And almost wanted to ask. But he respected his old man too much. Hightailing out of Harlem for the Q-Borough before his son was tainted by the poverty stricken surrounding had a lot to do with that. It was his dream to raise productive children with the potential to become President.

"Wanna go catch a movie?" he asked Action. "Maybe play some video games, then go get some new sneaks from Green Acres?"

Action asked, "Just you and me?" as he picked up his cigar from the floor.

"Uncle Destro and Zac don't go anywhere with us anymore. And I don't like the new guys."

"What about your mother, would you like her to come?"

"Guess A.J. doesn't know that out play-play uncles were killed, huh daddy?" Katrina spat as she and Iris strutted pass headed for her bedroom.

"Hey, Mr. Anwar," said Iris, waving and a little shocked by her friends sentiments.

"Hey Iris," Action replied looking pass her smile and at his daughter's frown. "And you Katrina. We need to talk."

Katrina did a 180 degree turn, lifted her shades, said, "About what? Smacking me for no reason?"

"Pop, what is Katrina talking about?"

"Listen son, why don't you take Iris downstairs and make

her one of your famous ice cream sundaes, while I have a word with your sister."

A.J. grabbed hold of Iris' hand and led her down the spiral staircase back to the ground floor.

"What's your problem? Your mother lets you go away for a week and you come back a different person? You don't say shit like that around your little brother."

Before she could reply, he went on to say, " And that stunt you pulled last night – you dead wrong."

"No, you're wrong! You kept us sheltered, you lied to us, and you assume that we'll always be naïve. What are you gonna tell him when he grows up and finds out our," – she tittered – "uncles were killed in the line of your fire?"

Action looked her up and down, said, "You think you really know what the fuck is going on, don't you? There are people out there dying for the day to hurt my people!"

"For what? Why?"

"You got some nerve!"

"Now why would people want to hurt your people? No, why are they dying to hurt your people?"

"Katrina, you're dead wrong!"

"I know one thing, it's like you don't wanna see me happy. Probably'd rather see me like mommy. Know what though – I want to be nothing like her! I wanna live! Experience life!" she told her father, her voice rising an octave with each syllable.

"That's an insult. Your mother is an exceptional woman! Did a hell of a job raising you and your brother!"

Katrina shook her head in disgust. "She's a housewife. She has no life. No, better yet, a home attendant. You two don't even share the same room! Haven't in years. Why would I want to be like her.

"What?"

"I don't want to be like her!"

"Well, you should," he replied, blowing smoke from his mouth. "The kind of woman you want to be, they're expendable."

"Expendable?"

"Yeah, easily replaceable. Relationships that'll be brief and more sexual than anything. Once he uses you up, he'll get rid of you. Send you back to your daddy. That's if he doesn't turn you out on drugs first, then pimp you out to his boys."

A statement like that should've cut deep, woke her up. But it didn't; it made her more rebellious. "I'm sexually active now, by the way. And for once I'm doing me without worrying what you'll think. Or what you may do."

"WHAT?!"

"And maybe you only kept her around to raise us. Daddy, it takes a village to raise a child."

Action added more fire to his cigar, puffed a bit, then said, "Well I'll be damned, you not only came back deflowered, but you got a degree in psychology too. You're all grown up and so opinionated. Maybe we should've been sent you away! Maybe it's time for you to move on!"

"What's going on, Anwar? Katrina, what are you two fussing about?" Drenae quizzed from the far end of the hall where the master bedroom was located.

"Sorry, if we disturbed you. We'll keep it down," Action returned.

"Okay," Drenae replied.

As soon as her mother was back in the confines of her room, Katrina said, "If you want me to leave, I will."

Action glared at the memorable moments lining the wall in the corridor. As his orbs bounced from frame to frame, he traveled a time line. Katrina's time line. From her kindergarten flicks to her high school graduation photos, caps and gowns, class pictures. It was all there. So much to be proud of. But now he had no idea who she was, where she was headed, or just how much shame she would bring him. What he did know was she'd taken a bite of that rotten apple and tasted the worm.

"I want you to leave here," he finally said.

Katrina was stunned. "Leave?"

"Leave the car too."

"That's my car though!"

"Bought with my money," he reminded her.

"You just gonna Indian give?"

"Leave the house keys too. You can ring the doorbell when you visit," were his last words.

EIGHTEEN

"Y ou want some of this big homie?" asked BB, his hand extended with a burning blunt in it.

"Nah, I'm straight," Capri replied as he led the way through Washington Heights, across the bridge and into the Bronx.

Zest and Stink weren't far behind, both their cars carrying a little extra muscle. A few other homies picked up the rear, following closely. Since the matter was one of serious circumstances, each car had a walkie-talkie. Using the information Christine provided, Capri had the crew right in Tackhead's hood which Capri realized was Nitti's as well. As they drove through, the young cats flanking the corners sent shells with their eyes. Non fitting the description given. And there was no sign of the Benz wagon. Capri pulled over by Warren's Café on University Ave, got out. Everyone else followed suit.

"Murda, I want y'all to scour this shit. That means Andrews Ave, Montgomery, 174th Street, 175th Street. Featherbed Lane. Anything look suspicious, y'all know what it is—"

"Red wolves is howling!"

After driving around for a while, they lucked up. A call came in. The Benz was being toweled off by a bum on 171st and Macombs Road. Naturally, Capri thought of Daffany since she lived right on that bloc. Had it not been about life or death for his homie, he'da paid her a visit. Instead, momentum and his rugged nature had him hop out his 850 and walk right up on the scrawny bum.

"Yo, who paid you to wash this car?" he ask, the importance of the answer written all over his face.

But the bum wasn't intimidated. Having been born and raised in the Bronx, and an addict for nearly two decades, he'd seen everything but the face of God, and done everything but commit suicide. And he didn't think he was doing anything wrong. So he said, "Why, you try'na het that Black Man's Wish toweled off next?"

Before he knew what hit him, Zest had leaped from his coupe and slapped him.

"Oh shit! He smacked blood out that nigga, Blood!" BB laughed, the severity of the situation gone for a brief moment.

"Who paid you to wash the car?" Zest snapped, hand cocked back again.

"Tall kid, got a little girl by chickie on the third floor, man."

"What building, nigga?!"

"1515 Macombs Road," he rushed out, his eardrum ringing crazy and his heartbeat pounding.

All Capri could do was shake his head. The world had just gotten smaller. He dialed Daffany's number, and as he expected, Nitti picked up.

"This Capri, come downstairs."

"I ain't at my moms' spot," Nitti shot back.

"I know; you in 151. Third floor. Come downstairs."

Three stories above, Nitti crept to the window, his mind so twisted that he'd forgotten his baby mama lived in a back apartment until he peeked out and saw a brick wall staring back at him. "Gimme a minute," he told Capri.

"I ain't got all day, bee."

Nitti grabbed his jacket and headed for the door. Only he didn't go downstairs, he went up on the roof. There he stood overlooking a significant portion of the Bronx. From where he stood he could see Yankee Stadium, the 161st Street Bridge, the tracks the 4-train raced north and south on, countless tenements, and then the sight he didn't want to see. Capri huddled up with some formidable figures. Unforgettable niggas.

Downstairs Capri grew impatient. "Zest, go around back. Stink and BB, come on."

Capri shot into the building, up the stairs to a place he was familiar with. Nitti was on his way down the back fire escape when he peeped Zest standing below, and started back up. Zest climbed up onto the extended ladder and gave chase. The apartment door was unlocked so Capri took a gander to find out Nitti was gone. When he exited BB and Stink was walking off the elevator.

"Come on, the roof!" Capri suggested.

There Nitti was, climbing back over the ledge.

"I said come downstairs, not up nigga!"

Nitti said, "I can explain."

"This lame got me climbing up fire escapes, fuckin' my Versace jeans up and all that!" Zest spazzed as he dusted himself off.

"How'd you get the car, Nitti?" Capri said getting straight to the point.

Nitti said, "My baby moms?"

"What?" they all said, confused.

"My baby moms! I know! I heard you on the answering machine!"

"Don't try and make this about her. You know I don't rock like that. You know why the fuck I'm here. How'd you get the car? Where's my lil' man?"

With the quickness BB patted Nitti down, dug his pockets, and came up with a diamond encrusted bone Bones keep his keys assembled on. BB lifted them above his head, said, "This nigga's food."

With his eyes planted on young BB, Nitti said, "Wait!" he knew he wasn't fucking with some soggy corn flake niggas. He also knew that could be his very last day in the jungle unless he saved himself. "Scarface Dave snatched your man. Did it for Tackhead. That's all I know."

It didn't take much persuading to get Nitti to get Dave on the phone. A couple of pages, and Dave was all ears. "What up, you finish getting the car washed?"

"Yeah. When you coming to get it?"

"Soon!"

"Yo, I got somewhere to be."

"Aiight. Bust it, that kid that was fucking your chick, I was suppose to end his career today. But he got low on me."

"Word?"

"Word! I'm coming to get the car."

"I'll be here," Nitti said, hanging up. He then turned to his captors and said, "He's on his way. White GTI."

At gun point, Zest led Nitti down the staircase. Stink, Capri, and BB exited the building first, heat tucked under their leathers. They moved as though the two lovebirds seated on the stoop weren't even there. But the chick and her man let it be known they saw nothing by trooping up the hill, never looking back.

"Be easy, dick," Zest told Nitti, the Ruger in his side.

Capri looked for any sign of the GTI before saying, "Yo, Zest sit him across the street in that park. We gonna move the cars to Jerome Ave. Easy route to the Deegan if shit get messy."

Zest tossed BB his keys, said, "A scratch, you bought it lil' nigga!"

They parked up and came right back. A few minutes later the GTI pulled up on some chrome rims that appeared to be too big. Out slid a dark skin kid in a black army jacket with his Dodgers cap pulled low.

"That's him right there," Nitti announced feeling like Judas. "Y'all can let me go now, right?"

Nitti was ignored. All focus was on Dave, mainly the bulge on the right side of his jacket. Capri backed out a brand new calico and tapped BB, then high stepped back across the busy two way. Traffic paused. The driver of an old compact car honked his horn. Someone in another vehicle shouted, "Ass hole!" more horns blared at an alarming rate.

Scarface Dave spun around to see what the commotion was. At first it looked like nothing. But then he recognized Carpi. Bronx bred, he knew drama when he seen it and acted accordingly by lifting the Uzi from his jacket and letting the gunshots blow. The rapid fire created the sound of combat as windows shattered, voices shrilled, and shells found their way through the innocent.

Capri threw BB to the asphalt then popped back. Caught in the crossfire, a woman could only think of the young children strapped into their baby seats in the back of her car. Panic stricken, she rammed her way out of the battlefield, oblivious to damage she was doing. Her heroics left young BB's frail frame crushed, having been rolled over several times. Capri saw his ravaged body, then the automobile fleeing on the sidewalk.

Zest notice Capri was distracted and Dave was about to seize the moment once he had flipped his clip, so he picked up the slack. As he approached squeezing both his Rugers, Stink raised the Dessert to Nitti's neck and splattered his larynx and windpipe all over the park bench leaving Nitti behind to drown on his own blood. Stink then joined his comrades on some militant shit releasing a barrage of hollow heads at Dave's Dodger cap.

Dave ducked behind a car and returned fire, eventually lodging some hot shit in one of his attackers.

"I'm hit!" Stink groaned, the sound of sirens nearing.

"Hold me down," Capri shouted tossing Stink's arm over his shoulder and rushing him to their cars.

"I'm damn near empty!" Zest returned. "And the cops is coming!"

Dave continued his onslaught, didn't stop firing until he peeped an unoccupied vehicle with the engine running.

Grinning, he hopped in and took off. Dragging Stink to the car, Capri looked back to see Dave fleeing, the stolen car speeding over BB's limp body like he was a bump in the road. He knew they'd fucked up. That they'd never see Bones alive again. That this karma wasn't the result of his generosity.

NINETEEN

A significant portion Stink's blood was all over the passenger seat of Capri's car. But he wasn't dead. Rosa, his main squeeze, contacted a family friend as soon as she got the news. His forte was lypo and implants, so nipping and tucking a gunshot victim would be easy, Rosa figured when Capri told her they weren't going to the hospital. Instead of asking questions she had him there and ready to operate when Capri sped up in their New Jersey backyard. For a small fee the Dominican fellow gave Stink some pain killers then removed both bullets that'd lodged in his hip and abdomen.

While Stink rested, Capri paid the tab. He wanted to be out there searching for Bones instead of being the victim of pity, but word was caps was crawling. So he had to sit and wonder. Wonder why? What went wrong? What would people think when word got out that he'd push BB to his death.

"What happened?" Rosa quizzed once the plastic surgeon was gone.

"What did he tell you?" Capri returned unable to make eye contact.

"That someone tried to jack y'all while y'all were getting the cars washed. But I didn't believe that." Her hands were on her hips and her eyes were all over Capri. When he lifted his head Rosa thought the man hadn't slept all week.

"Then that's what happened."

"So why didn't you take him to the emergency room, or wait for an ambulance?"

"Too complicated."

Rosa wasn't the type of chick who could be easily fooled. And she was never given anything in life. She'd earned it all, including Stink's honor, respect, and loyalty. Sharing the same bed with him for five years was more than enough time to know when he was and wasn't being truthful. He was the man she planned to marry one day, then bear this children, so she had no intentions of losing him to the streets. At a beautiful five-foot-nine, the Latina leaned on the island separating the kitchen and the lounge area, and asked Capri, "You got a girl, right?"

"I have a fiancée," he replied.

"Wow, I didn't take you for the proposing type."

"What did you take me to be?"

"I really don't know you that well, but from what I do know, not the type to put a ring on it."

"She deserves it."

"What? The ring? Or a life long partner who'll lover her unconditionally for all of her days and nights?"

Capri said, "All the above – in a perfect world."

"In a perfect world, huh?" Rosa retorted. "When he wakes up I'm taking him away. Hedonism II."

"Where is that?"

"A resort in Negril, Jamaica." She ran her fingers through her curly mane, the nudist element bringing a smirk to her mental. "That man in there, I love more than I love my mother. He comes home every night. Calls me during the day. Sends me flowers to my job. Leaves me notes when he's gonna be late. He even cooks for me. Hotdogs, eggs, waffles, hero sandwiches – but it's the thought that wows me."

"A gangsta and a gentleman, huh?" As soon as Capri said that, Stink appeared moving gingerly.

"I did the best I could cleaning that mess up, bee. Not the best, but forensics wouldn't find shit if they tried," he told

Capri, grimacing.

"You're suppose to be resting, baby," Rosa said, "not cleaning interiors."

The phone rang.

"Get that, ma," Stink told her, taking a seat on the stool right across from Capri.

"I know you hear me Marcel!" Rosa snapped. "You should be resting, recovering. You were shot, papi!"

"What, I suppose to be moping around here? Hell no! emotions are a health hazard in our world!"

"And I am scared for you. Because I know there is more to this story."

"Rosa, the phone."

Rosa rolled her eyes, sucked her teeth, but eventually stomped her way to the ringing. "It's your father!" she shouted, coming back towards them. She took a seat right next to Stink, handed him the cordless.

"What up, pop?"

"I'm goo, Insha Allah. The Prophet, may peace and blessing be upon him, was recorded to have said, 'I am amazed at the believer's situation. His situation is always good. If something occurs to him that pleases him, he praises Allah, and this is good for him. And if something occurs to him that displeases him, and he is patient, it is good for him. No one else's situation is always good except the believer's.'"

Stink was stuck. At a time as challenging as the one he and his crew were facing, his pops called preaching patience. He wasn't trying to hear that. He was ready to go full throttle. Make some more niggas bleed.

"So what else is going on?"

"Your lady tells me your health ain't what it was before you left home this morning."

Stink turned to Rosa, glared as he said, "I'm straight."

"Listen. My arms are short right now, but if there's anything I can do, let me know."

"As a matter of fact, there is." He turned away from Rosa. "The ball buster."

"Yeah."

"Time to go. Twenty-five sound fair?"

"What's understood needs no explanation. What's up, your brother straight too?"

"I'ma call him as soon as I hang up with you," he told his father as he watched Rosa saunter off towards the kitchen.

"And I'll call you this weekend, son. Peace."

"Peace."

Marcel Sr. hung up with a pay day in sight, and Stink with some pain to kill. He popped two more Tylenol's, then punched some number into the cordless. While it rang, Stink asked Capri, "Where Zest at?"

"His moms' spot."

"He's cool?"

"The question is, are you cool?"

Stink took in some air, exhaled said, "My Jag is still on Jerome Ave, some nigga I don't even know put some balls in me, and I watched a little homie get crushed by a car, but umm, I feel better than I did an hour ago."

Capri was about to say something when Stink put up a hand and said, "He picked up."

"What's poppin' bro? heard it got real messy out there?"

"Yeah. I probably end up with a limp."

"Naaah! Say word?!"

"Word up," Stink replied, before adding, "I'm good though. Zest cool, Pri G-mackin', but umm, BB didn't make it back. And we still ain't got no lead on Bones."

"I ain't felling that!"

"Who you with?"

"730," Murda said, speeding around a livery cab doing the limit.

"Listen, the Jag is on 172nd and Jerome. Go scoop it."

"We on it, bro. we on Featherbed Lane right now, at the

light on University. And it look like some niggas on that corner right there by them projects. Want us to put it in--?"

"Nah, go get the car. Now! My prints is –"

The line went dead.

"Stink was almost killed," Murda told 730. And instead of flowing orders, 730 demanded they park up and pop the trunk. They then brazenly strolled onto University Avenue unable to conceal the artillery they possessed. The skies were still pretty clear, and the Ave had a lot of activity. But, 730 a stone cold gangbanger loyal to his oaths, his prayers and his hood, didn't give two shits. "Hold me down!" he ordered running across the intersection on University. Once he reached the divider, he let the modified AK-47 do the talking.

The chopping sound of the assault weapon caused massive damage, but not before the chaos. Bystanders scrambled, screamed, shouted, shuffled and shoved for their lives. It was every man and woman for himself as they tried defying 730's logic, the flares coming at them. But the slugs started connecting. Bodies began to drop, flip, and flop.

"Yo, it's bitches over there!" Murda shouted, his gun still cold.

"So!' 730 responded, his finger mashing the trigger.

The casualties were piling up, and Murda found himself panicking. He knew the severity of conspiracy. The time it carried. He felt powers lurking. All the things that could go wrong. "Come on! That's enough! Po-nine be here any minute!" Murda pled, his eyes surveying the scene. But he never saw what was coming.

Just as 730 ceased fire, tucked the AK, Lava emerged from a tenement palming the rubber grip of a .44 magnum with an inferred beam atop it. Scarface Dave was right on his heels with that Uzi in tow. Lava sat a red dot on 730's face and tugged on the trigger a couple times.

"Bloom! Bloom!" was the sound.

"Oooh shit!" Murda released as 730's blood, nose, teeth,

165

right eye and skull fragments splattered his face, fitted and the sleeve of his crimson Yankees jacket. 730's body went limp, smacking the pavement like a tree in a lumberyard.

Bypassing the panic from seeing his homie slaughtered, Murda dropped to a knee behind a idle vehicle and returned fire. "Come in! one, two. One, two!" he heaved into a walkie-talkie he was holding, hoping anyone would holla back.

Lava and Scarface Dave had him pinned behind a car just waiting for him to come up. Murda tried to scramble for the AK, but Dave delivered rapid fire into 730's lifeless frame. Murda quickly scooted back to safety, planting his back against the car. As the vastly approached smelling victory in the air, Murda could hear the shots getting closer and louder. He just knew they were coming for him, that the end was near. He looked up, his semi-auto aimed in their direction. Lava saw that red baseball cap and threw two at Murda's head while his cohort continued creeping. Murda looked up into the skies, said a prayer. He looked to the corner store bodega ready to dash for the front door. Even wondered where the cops were. Why they hadn't arrived yet. "Not like this," he sadly released.

"What up?" escaped the walkie-talkie.

"Yo! I'm on University stuck behind a fucking car with these niggas gunning at me! You hear me???"

"Which side?"

"It's a cab base on this side! You hear me?"

"Yeah, I'm coming now homie!" Rocko assured.

"Hurry up! This nigga got a beam and his man got some automatic shit."

Rocko could hear the gunplay. And as he shot up Featherbed Lane, people raced by to safety leading him right to the scene. But he couldn't locate Murda or the shooter, too much havoc. Then he peeped two cats in black hoodies.

Murda spotted the cherry red M5 spin the corner. On his hands and knees he scurried from the sidewalk and was nearly rundown by a speeding van. The MPV swerved and that's when

Rocko peeped Murda and threw it in reverse.

The red Tahoe came zooming down the other side of the street, guns sticking out the window. Seeing that small window of opportunity, Murda crawled towards the slowing M5 as the passenger door swung open and leaped to safety.

As fate would have it, just as authorities were pulling up to the carnage, the M5 was headed in the opposite direction. By the time they got to Jerome Avenue, the Jaguar car was being lifted onto a flatbed with a feral agent behind the wheel. And just a block away the Benz wagon was being confiscated by the FBI.

TWENTY

P rincess was still mourning the debacle of her relationship, and questioning her courage as a woman. Every once in a while the phone would ring and it would be one of her clients checking on her and asking when could Diva's Galore expect her to be back behind the desk guiding the careers of video vixens. She had some of the baddest models in the New York tri-state area working the cameras as the eye candy for some of the most notable rappers and crooners in the music biz. And a few of the print models weren't far from the runway. But she'd keep it brief by saying, "Soon."

With no one who could really relate on speed dial, or a decent enough lie to justify the breakup, she turned to her only friends. The ones in her head.

The first voices emerged around the time she was sixteen after being forced upon by the man who eventually became her first love. He was a smooth talking, slick cat with a lot of influence, and already old enough to legally drink. His aggression and transgressions turned a naïve, easily impressionable girl with so many aspirations into a shell just wandering through her improvised surroundings. Then one day this breathy voice with the sexy undertone emerged and said, "Stop moping! You wanted it! Nobody told you take his money or buy them little ass shorts with it! So suck it up, and make yourself seen before he finds something else young and tender," when the contrary was true.

The inception of the second voice wasn't far behind, sounding sweet and sassy, poetic and major. It said, "Don't get caught up though. Just use what you got to get what you want!" not only did she get caught up, but for the next sixteen years the voices in her head were constant and dependable in times of distress. But it wasn't them she wanted, it was her young don...Zest.

Having done everything required of her as a woman, she was sure the good would outweigh the bad and Zest would forgive her and return home. She gave good head, loved anal, cooked, cleaned and knew how to get money. But hours began to feel like days, days like weeks, and naturally reality settled in. He wasn't coming back.

Restless and sick of watching old Pam Grier movies, she decided to step out, go for a stroll through midtown Manhattan and get some sun in her life. She was never drop dead gorgeous, that she admitted for the first time when she got to the mirror. But she always knew how to accentuate her advantages. The killer shape, smooth mocha brown skin and chinky eyes. That thick dark hair that laid perfectly, and them juicy lips that poked out like her hips. Didn't take her much time to get ready being as though she had no one to fascinate and wow, still being fairly knew to the predominantly white neighborhood. Dressed for the occasion – jeans, sneakers, a t-shirt, a visor, sunglasses over her eyes – she vacated the Central Park West apartment for the first time in about a week. Thoughts of the suicide attempt resurfaced. Zest's hand around her throat as she lay exhausted in her hospital bed came to mind. Then Bill's demands. Her very own triangle of sin.

As she was about to greet the sun, trying to get back to the living, she peeped two cats with distinct features approaching her. Black and assertive. They were enforcers. Of the law.

"Princess Quinnones?"

"Yes, who are you?" she asked if the bulk of the vests

169

beneath their clothing and the shields dangling from their necks didn't already provide that information.

"FBI. We'd like to have a word with you."

She took a gander at the credentials he brandished glared in his green eyes, said "How can I help you, Agent McCants?"

"Bornsavior Quinnones, any relation to you?"

"No," Princess said shaking her head and wondering what her brother had gotten himself into.

"Well, we have a car in custody that we know he used to drive. It's registered to you."

"What do you mean, used to drive? Is he in some kind of trouble?"

Agent Atkins said, "Ms. Quinonez, your brother's dead. His body was discovered early this morning in Aqueduct Park, an exit wound in the back of his head."

The Chanel clutch Princess once held tightly slipped from her fingertips as everything around her began to lose speed. The yellow cabs, the pigeons, the patrons, and of course the lips of the federal agents all moved in slow motion.

"He was just one of many murdered yesterday."

One of many...

...murdered yesterday.

Yesterday.

Yesterday.

"Dead???"

"Execution style. We'd like to ask you a few questions," McCants stated hating to be the bearer of the bad news. "Maybe you –"

With tears building in her chinky eyes, Princess knelt down for her clutch and rushed back into the building. The ride back to the fourteenth floor was a long one, the voices in her head suggesting her Zest was responsible. That Capri was his accomplice.

Once inside she raced to the bar, poured some vodka down her throat straight out the bottle, all logic lost to emotion.

The phone rang startling her.

She thought it would be one of her clients, but the caller said, "Comstock Correctional Facility shift commander. Is Ms. Quinonez in?"

"This is her."

"You're listed as William Giles' emergency contact. I'm sorry to inform you that he was fatally stabbed in the prison yard this morning. The security team's still investigating."

"Dead? Billy??? My Billy?" she stammered, falling to her knees.

"I'm sorry. But as I stated, a full investigation is being conducted. What would you like done with his remains?"

"I, I don't know," Princess muttered then hung up sensing that her life was too in danger. She paced, bottle in hand, paranoia sinking in. peeking out the window, she contemplated her next move.

Downstairs the agents thought about following her, and was about to until they got a call from their supervisor ordering them to return to the station.

Turned out they had a witness willing to spill his guts, and destined to give somebody a life sentence. In addition, the Benz wagon and the Jaguar were being swept for fingerprints. Trent could feel things about to unravel, and his future son-in-law being caught up in that tide that was about to wipe out half of Harlem's underworld. Agent Atkins was prepping himself for the interview, having never been part of such a huge case, but was quickly sidelined when Trent said, "I'll conduct the interview, you check on those cars we picked up."

When Trent got to the interview room there sat a small, gnome like looking cat with a smile as wide as the table he had his filthy hands resting on. Most of his teeth were gone, his eyes were no longer white and half his right iris was torn. It was a wonder he could see anything. Though he didn't exactly conform with the typical government witness, Trent wasted no time probing the fella with no mystery to his agenda.

"So what'd you say your name was again?"

"Maurice Banks. But everybody knows me as Mo B. Dick. I assume you know how I got the name," he cackled.

"And why are you here again? I mean, what is it that you would like to report, and possibly testify to?"

"Well, I'm the cat that was washing the Benzo when them niggas pulled up."

"So it was more than one?"

"It was three. Three of 'em. No, four. They all had guns. And ah, one got run over by a car."

Trent took a seat atop the table. "What were they driving?"

"A black BMW, a Jaguar, and another Benz. Silver."

"Okay," Trent said relieved he hadn't said a black Hummer.

"They were the shooters."

"So you can identify the shooters?"

"Sure! I seen when they hauled Franc out the building."

"How'd you know it was Franc? And how'd they know where to find Franc?"

"I told them."

"So you pointed them in the right direction?"

Mo B Dick nodded, said, "It's not the way you're making it sound."

"What else did you see?"

"The cat in the Volkswagen pull up with the machine pistol and start firing."

Volkswagen. Machine pistol. "He fired first?"

"And last! About a hunned! He took 'em all on. By himself. Even shot one of 'em. The one who got out the Jag."

Trent didn't remember seeing that in the report. "Someone else was shot other than Franco?"

"Dark skin cat, lotta jewelry, and a mouth full of gold and diamond, red rubies."

"there was only one body on the scene."

"They took him with them."

"Who?"

"The Bloods."

Trent looked up, met him at the eyes. "I'm going to show you a book of mug shots. Think you can pick these cats out if you see them again?"

"What's in it for me?" Mo B Dick quipped.

"What did my supervisor tell you?"

"Robo cop told me for truthful information I would be taken care of handsomely. And for starters, some Cheese Doodles, a Twix, and some Coke would be nice."

Trent let himself out the interview room.

"Bring some ice with that!!!"

Trent left and was back in a flash. He sat the snacks on the table said, "Now where were we?"

"You were suppose to show me some pictures. So I can finish this interview and get my lady out."

"Right. What exactly is your lady in for?"

"Receiving stolen property," Mo B. Dick replied with both a Twix and Doodles in his mouth.

Trent slid the book across the table and sat at the other end until Mo B Dick was done stuffing his face. "Let's do this," he said grabbing hold of the thick binder. He flicked through every page, a different facial expression for each one. but when Trent would say "What?", he'd respond with, "I was locked up with him somewhere before."

And just when Trent was growing restless and impatient, the man pointed, fingering someone. "It was him! I can never forget that buck-fifty on the side of his face!"

"Let me see," Trent commanded as he grabbed the book.

"The light skin one with the curly blowout," Mo B. Dick said, pointing.

Of all the faces plastered throughout the binder he fingered one of the most feared men in the whole array. No. 031. Capri Hayward.

"You sure this man killed—"

"I ain't say he killed nobody," Mo B. Dick halted for a

moment, sipped his Coke, then said, "But he was there. I was talking to him when his man slapped the taste out my mouth."

Trent had to think quick or his soon son-in-law was about to become an accomplish to first degree murder. And his daughter would be torn, or worst…a prisoner's wife. In a voice that sounded unfamiliar to him, he said, "Impossible, he's locked up right now."

"And I'm the leader of the free world," Mo B Dick chuckled. "That's him. I know what the fuck I saw with these eyes. It was him leading the pack! I ain't crazy."

"I'm telling you. I arrested him myself. You said you were locked up with half the men in this book. That's probably one."

"Is you shitting me??? It was him, on my block. I seen him!"

"If you wanna get that lady of your out, I suggest you go back in the book."

Mo B. Dick began to question himself, wondering if he was experiencing temporary blindness again. He thought of Lola, his lady of twenty years, smoking a rock with her, then trekked through the photos again, and when he got to Capri's mug shot he stopped and stared, said, "I ain't crazy. It's him. But you saying you locked him up like niggas don't make bail."

Trent couldn't believe it himself, but he seethed it. "Picked another photo."

The door opened and both men saw an opportunity to do someone some good slipping away. In walked Agent Atkins. Behind him was Agent Jackson, his massive physique a think of precision.

Neither knew how much was heard, or if anything at all. And then in a whimsical manner, Mo B. Dick said, "That's him right there."

"Where, which one?" Agent Jackson burrowed in.

Mo B. Dick pointed, and Agent Jackson said, "Joseph Abrams??? That's the one you saw kill Franc Locket, and shove that sixteen year old kid up on that car????"

"MmmHmm," Mo B Dick replied, nodding had nappy head.

Agent Jackson gave him a pen and paper, said, "Write down the name of your girlfriend, and we'll have her out tonight."

"So this is how the system works?" asked Mo B Dick feeling like a worthless rat. He'd never imaged himself in a situation as such, and once upon a time frowned up that type of craftiness. Even participated in some rat bashing back in his day. As he scribbled down his woman's name, he inwardly cursed himself.

"Atkins, process the paperwork and send it over to the ADA in the Bronx. McCants, let me have a word with you, out here."

Trent made eye contact with Mo B. Dick, then exited the interview room. With the door closed, and Atkins on his way.to a phone, Agent Jackson said, "It's not his m.o. He's not gang related. Their crew are more so a black mob. And I'm willing to guarantee that his fingerprints aren't anywhere on neither of the two vehicles we confiscated.

Fully prepared for that, Trent rebutted, "There was a Volkswagen on the scene. That may've been the car he arrived in."

"Do we have a Volkswagen???"

"No but I do have pictures of Abrams handing a known gang member a bag of money. If the shaking hands doesn't make a nexus, then I don't know what does."

"Let me see these pictures."

Lo and behold, Trent had the pictures on hand. Jackson took a glance, and though he didn't have a good feeling about it, he wanted to see where it would lead. "We'll run it by the attorney general, get an arrest warrant, then pick him up. If we're lucky, he'll hand us Action. Nice work."

"It's a start."

"That means there's a finish near. However, you know there was four killed and five wounded yesterday on University, right? One, a fifteen year old kid, was left with a macerated kidney, completely liquefied! And who's from University?"

175

"Franc Locket."

"One of the deceased, the man with the AK-47, is a resident of Harlem, and a gang member."

"Okay."

"And where was Quinonez, another Harlem kid, discovered?"

"The park on University."

"What happened with the sister? You know she has a file, right? Was almost indicted back in the 80s."

"We made contact, but—"

Agent Jackson tossed his huge arm over Trent's shoulder like they were chums, said, "When you're done wrapping this up, see what she knows! After all, that was her brother. And I'll remember you when I get where I'm going."

TWENTY ONE

"Patience, the phone!"

"Mom, who is it?"

"Christine."

"Who?!"

"Christine."

"Dad, don't move. I'll be right back."

"I gotta get back in the field, baby girl."

"I can take this call, and we can still finish our conversation."

"How about this weekend? I should be free. Maybe we can grab some ice cream like we used to do when you were a little girl."

"I'd like that."

"Sometimes I still can't believe that you're twenty-three."

"Or that I'm engaged, huh?"

Trent hesitated. "Or that you're engaged. I mean, as a parent I just want the best for you."

"I want your support in this, but if I don't get it, I'll understand. You just understand, I'm going through with it. He's the love of my life. The best for me."

"I support you then," Trent professed. That wasn't something that came easy for him. But botching the investigation did. And he wondered just what else he was capable of.

"It was nice to have you home for dinner," Mrs. Mary told

Trent as she handed Patience the phone before perching herself on his lap.

"It's nice being home."

Patience smiled inside and out hoping that when she and Capri were in their 40s they'd still be together and as into each other as her parents were. Letting herself out onto the sun porch, she said, "Christine, who?"

"Took you long enough!"

Patience glared at the phone then put it back to her face, asked, "Who is this?"

"Princess."

"That's who I thought it was. Why'd you tell my mother your name was Christine?"

"Because I gotta tell you about Christine, girl, " Princess shot back grinning.

Patience felt like she was talking to a stranger. "Why would you have to tell me about someone I don't know? And why you sound like that?"

"Like what?"

"All sassy and shit."

"I don't know, but what I do know is we need to get up so I can put you on to your newest competition."

Patience took a seat, crossed her leg, laughing.

"What you laughing at?"

"You. You call my house playing games. What, you bored?"

"Bored? When I'm bored I get my vibrator out."

Patience sensed the seriousness and asked, "So there really is a Christine?"

"Yes there is, and she's sucking your man's dick."

Patience got queasy, stomach monkey flipping. She could no longer sit, found herself taking in too much air, her throat tightening as were her fists. She paced, then out came, "How you know this?"

"The same way I know you won't give him head."

I don't deserve this. And she doesn't deserve my man. I did the bids with him. I gave him nine years of my life."

"That's not it."

Patience released a burst of air, said, "What else?"

"You gotta promise me you won't put me in this."

With very little thought Patience said, "I promise!"

"He got her knocked up."

"Pregnant???"

"Last time I checked that what knocked up meant."

Patience cringed, depraved thoughts came to mind.

"If I was you I'd cut that lil' bitch face."

"You know where she lives?"

"Yeah. What you doing tomorrow?"

"I gotta work, but I'm free around three."

"At three-thirty meet me by the Planetarium right there on 84th Street."

"Just make sure you're there," Patience sneered, unable to remember the last time she had a fight. And then without even saying bye, she disconnected the call. Fingers trembling, she dialed right back out. It rang, and it rang, and then, "Hello."

"Where you at, Capri???"

He was in the projects lounging on a park bench drunk off Hennessy, preparing to light up his second blunt to the head. As if all the death surrounding him wasn't enough – BB, Bones, 730, Nickels – all his young troops were at each other's throats tearing deeper into his troubled soul. The money and the success had gone to their heads. Wildlife and Lansky were thinking about going into business for themselves, and happened to say it in front of the wrong person. Diamond and Purple were mad at Christine for telling Capri, mad at her for implicating Tyanna in Bones' murder, and thought she needed a reality check in the form of a flawless bitch smack. Zest got word of the whole thing and suggested doing them dirty then running them all out of Harlem. But Capri knew they weren't ready for that type of pain. So instead of exposing them, he decided to change the culture, inspiring their entrepreneurial spirit as long as they remained tight knit and copped off them. "No backbiting, no slandering, and no tripping on each other."

Right after he'd gave his demands and all agreed, a short scrawny woman with a raunchy switch walked up on them. She was wearing some dingy jeans, a disfigured sweater that had lost all its luster, her nipples poking out like antennas do to the plummeting temperatures. Capri could tell she was once a beauty before the drugs got hold of her. "What's up, y'all doing something?" she directed at Capri. When no one answered, she said, "I don't want no credit, I got money."

They'd all refused her once again.

Feeling rejected, she snapped. "Why the fuck won't y'all serve me?! Matter fact, where my son at? He'll serve me! BB, baby!" she called out.

It was at that moment that Capri had lost it. Chocked up with a heavy tear in his eye, he told her, "Your son's gone, Miss Banks."

"Gone where?" she quizzed, confused.

"Dead."

The woman could be heard throughout the projects screaming, "Where's my baby??? Who killed my baby???"

That led to the liquor, the weed, the park bench, his lonesome.

"Nigga, I know you hear me!" Patience screeched.

"Not right now. Tomorrow," he said hanging up, nearing a drunken stupor.

That just pissed Patience off even more.

The next day Patience left the fitness club minutes before Capri arrived to speak his peace. About 3:40 Princess spotted her nearing the Planetarium. Princess finished her cigarette, while waving her over.

"Come on, she sitting right down here. And she don't know you're coming," said Princess, beckoning for Patience to follow her.

Columbia Avenue was lined with parked cars, midday traffic was moving swiftly, but the pedestrians were far and few. Prime for some undetected lawlessness. Patience proceeded ready to do work, Princess matching her hurried pace. Suddenly the trunk of a black Lincoln popped open and out jumped Brother Joe and Baby Blue. Brother Joe slapped a wet cloth over Patience's mouth then forced her in the trunk. Blue slammed it shut, then got back in the car just as Action emerged from a late model sedan parked on the other side of the street.

"Princess," he snickered. "It's been a long time."

Princess, still a little inebriated, said, "I been around."

Amazed by Princess's ability to capture time, Action said, "If you didn't have that thing for young niggas, I might have a chance, huh?"

"Let's just keep this professional, please," Princess requested, though she couldn't help but think how easy it would be to rebound with a man like Action claiming her.

Action nodded, told Brother Joe, "Give her the bag, but first, tell me, why'd you cross your people?"

Princess sighed, pursed her lips. Words didn't come easy. And then that voice with the sexy undertone said, "Around here everybody's looking for something. And deception, disloyalty, and manipulation determines who lives and who doesn't. Now give me my money."

Action nodded again.

Brother Joe retrieved a brown bag from beneath the driver's seat, handed it to Princess tucked the bag under her arm while giving off a charming smile, then hit the nearest corner.

TWENTY TWO

BB lied still in his mahogany panel, gold latched casket, radiant crimson cushion beneath him, the best of garments gracing his body. White Armani silk with red buttons. On his feet, never before seen Uptowns, all red python skin. Of all those lost in this war of wits, none were sent off in better style. Capri had facilitated and funded the entire service. It was the first step in him attempt at accepting responsibility.

Miss Bank, BB's mother, moved about giving off this aura of strength, but deep down inside she was torn. Sober for the first in years, she watched people ranging from teachers to gangbabgers pay respects while wondering had her addiction attributed to his untimely death. She had no idea her son was so beloved. It was clear now why he'd joined the gang. To erase the sense of hopelessness. To be loved.

Trying to hold herself together, she noticed a familiar face, a dazzling one from her past. Working her three inch heels, she maneuvered her way over in the couture that came along with enough money to start a new life.

"Princess I didn't know you knew my son."

Princess was distracted, Zest under her watchful eye. She looked up wondering how she's been made. On her head was a black cowgirl had, and the collar of her jacket was sitting high.

"Princess," Miss Banks repeated.

"Cherel, hey," Princess clamored, the affect of years of drug abuse standing before her. "I'm sorry for you loss."

"I know my son was grown, but I didn't know he knew you. We went to school together."

"Don't forget, we ran in different crowds."

Miss Banks chuckled, said, "You ain't changed a bit."

"Yes, I have," Princess muttered. "I just had my little brother's flesh cremated yesterday. He knew yours on."

"No funeral?"

Princess shook her head. "When I'm done my work here in New York, I'll scatter his ashes in the ocean or something.

Having noticed a sneer on Princess' lips, and a switch in the pitch of her voice, she asked, "Are you Okay?"

Okay, I see Zest. There's Stink with the limp. Man-Man. Christine's here. But where's Capri???, Princess wondered, her eyes all over the place.

She must be stalking one of the young boys, thought Miss Banks.

"Why don't you find something to do," Princess suggested, tired of her hovering above her.

"If you're gonna be rude, you can leave!"

"Why don't you fall back, bitch. Stop fuckin' with me, please."

Miss Banks was furious now. "LEAVE!" she shouted looking for a little assistance.

And she got it.

"Miss Banks, who you talking to?" asked Zest, Stink and Man with him.

"It's nothing. I just wanted someone to leave."

"Who?"

"Princess."

"Princess is here?"

"Was here. Looks like she's gone."

Zest shot to the entrance, looking to convey his condolences for her loss, having tried contacting her on numerous occasions to no avail. By the time he got to the door there was no sign of her.

Princess was on 134th and Saint Nicholas. Out of breath. Her heartbeat thumping. She leaned back in her Range Rover, gathered herself while using the moonlight to punch ten digits into her phone.

"Peace!" she heard over some soft jazz after two rings.

"Bra, Brother Joe?"

"Yeah, what up?" he replied, one eye on the streets ahead and the other in the rearview. "Why you breathing so hard?"

"Let me," she stammered, exasperated, "catch my breath! I was at the wake. And, and there was no sign of Capri."

"Hold up. I'm being followed."

"By who?"

"Think it's the Feds. Two unmarked cars."

"So no what???"

"Stop asking so many damn questions!"

"We had a deal!" Princess snapped. "You's still own--!"

Click!

TWENTY THREE

In a loose and scatter tone, Iris said, "Capri, there they go." Her eagerness to please him was more transparent than ever. And Katrina's ambitions weren't far behind. While everyone was over at BB's wake, he was acting on a tip. He'd been tailing the target for about an hour now, just waiting for darkness to fall. They were in midtown, a half block from Saks Fifth.

Yes, there they were.

Tyanna was in a short fox jacket, fitted jeans, stylish stilettos, with a cute fedora on her head, plenty of bags in tow. And there he was, dragging his mink on the floor like a fat cat. He stopped, letting her go ahead as he fired up a blunt and watched her salacious strut. They didn't look like a concerned couple responsible for the murder of a made man. And that bother Capri. Like a soldier in the wild hunting a buffalo, this was a kill Capri wanted badly. It wasn't Action. And it would add nothing to his legacy, but it would mitigate a lot of pain.

On the other hand, Iris was preparing to live out yet another of her fantasies. And Katrina, coked the fuck up, couldn't believe she had a gun in her hand. She couldn't help but think back to that hot summer day at the basketball game when Tyanna had made her feel like a slouch, and couldn't wait to point and squeeze.

Strolling smoothly, Tackhead caught up with Tyanna and draped his arm around her neck flossing an icy watch and ring full of carats that made the studs in her ears look like diamond chips. They just knew the night belonged to them, that is until they heard the pitter patter of racing feet smacking the pavement. And as Capri expected, Tyanna dropped her bags and took off.

"Get her, girls!" Capri ordered closing in on Tackhead. In one shift motion Capri tool a razor sharp switchblade to Tackhead's stomach, dragging it from left to right, gutting him like the pig he was. He opened instantly. And as he reached for his stomach, his intestine fell into his hands. Capri raised his hand to open him again, and like music to his ears, he heard a series of gunfire.

SLASH!

Blood shot forth from Tack's jugular turning the top of his cream sweater burgundy. Stumbling backwards, mouth agape, he reached for his neck before eventually collapsing where he took his last breath. Rounding the corner was Tyanna minus the stilettos. She saw Capri waiting for her with open arms and shouted, "Noooo!"

He flipped that switchblade like an expert, ready to carve her up real nice too. But she doubled back, ran into the street, arms flailing and was speeding up Fifth Avenue. The impact of the hit sent Tyanna flying three stories high. She came down with a hard thud, and didn't budge.

"Come on, let's get out of here," Capri ordered watching as the yellow cab kept going, never looking back. The girls climbed into the van, but Capri doubled back for the watch and the jewels, the thick mitt in his pocket that unfurled as soon as he lifted it from Tackhead's pocket.

"Where we going now?" Katrina quizzed.

Capri just smiled. Smiled half the way back uptown. He thought of Daffany, and how hard he was going to slap her if they ever crossed paths again for playing him. Nitti, and how his career got cut short. Zest, and the Princess meltdown. Action, and how he would gut him. But never in a million years did he think he'd get a call, saying "Is my daughter with you? She hasn't been home in three days! She hasn't been to work. Didn't show up for our weekly lunch date at the Steak House on Central Park Ave. And—"

"What???"

"—I called Cheri's to see if she made her appointment, but they said she never showed up," Mary stammered, her voice rising with each syllable.

"That's not like her."

"Tell me something I don't know!" Mary deplored. "My daughter is missing!"

There was no escaping the fear in Mrs. Mary's voice. And it was clear to Capri that she wanted to know more than whether or not Patience was with him. That's when he decided it would be in his best interest not to mention stopping by the fitness club the other day even though she was gone when he got there.

"Capri!"

"Yeah."

"She could be hurt, or worst – dead."

"Don't' talk like that!" he begged, pulling over by a cab base. "Please, don't talk like that."

"I've been a homicide detective for eight years, in law enforcement for sixteen. It's ,y intuition. I can feel it when something is terribly wrong," she wept. "I'm about to call Trent, the report her missing."

Realizing Mary could have half the country on a manhunt with one phone call, placing all her friends, starting with him, under scrutiny, he said, "I'm on my way to Yonkers right now! Wait until I get there before you call anybody. I promise we'll find her."

"Okay," was all she could say, although she knew after 48 hours and no contact, no ransom, chances of seeing her daughter alive again were slim to none.

Capri tossed his phone onto the dash, busted a U-turn and sought the fastest way back to Harlem. Once there he stuck the girls in a safe-house, then hit the streets. There was no word on a kidnapping, no one had seen Action or anyone from his crew. After an hour of ruffling feathers and picking brains, he called Zest and Stink who happened to be a few blocks away on 115th Street discussing street politics.

"Blood, what's popping?" asked Stink as soon as Capri pulled up.

"What's good sun?" Zest questioned, still shocked to find out Stink had Will Bill pine boxed for his foulness, paying the tab and all.

Capri answered neither of his comrades. Only vapors escaped his mouth as he searched their faces for any possible larceny. When they looked the same way they did the last time he'd seen them, he said, "Patience is missing."

"What?" Zest quizzed, noticing a stain on Capri's sleeve. "What happened? You bleeding?"

Stink said, "Missing, missing?"

"I don't know. The other night she called me and I was on my bullshit. That was the last time I spoke to her. Then today right after I run down on that cat Tackhead, catch him slipping and wash him up, wifey moms call like, Patience is missing..."

Zest said, "Hold up, you caught the niggas Tack?"

"Y'all hear anything, let me know," Capri stated heading back to his car.

"I ain't never seen him like this," said Zest, hands grasping his belt buckle. "Never!"

"I don't like it, bee," Stink returned, leaned back against the public phone.

Sunk in the seat of his 850, Capri tried calling Patience. When she didn't answer, he just knew the tables had rotated. Hands wrapped around the steering wheel, he repeatedly pounded his forehead against the horn blaming himself for not protecting her.

Zest sighed, watching, wanting to do something. Everyone on the corner now knew something was terribly wrong. And then the 850 sped off.

Zest ran to his car, slammed it in first, Stink in the passenger seat, and trailed Capri. At that moment, they'da followed him into hell. Not even a red light could slow him down. And once he hit the Major Degan Expressway, he opened it up, didn't let up until he crossed Tuckahoe Avenue in Yonkers. Zest didn't miss a turn or a beat, never falling more than fifty feet behind.

Capri was switching lanes, putting the headers to work, weaving in and out of congestions with a reckless abandon. Finally, he parked, got out and stormed up the stairs.

Mrs. Mary was pacing the porch in a dark cardigan, some blue jeans, black Technica boots, and a face full of tears. Her arms were clutched across her chest as she fought off a light shiver. Capri tossed his arm over her shoulder, walked her inside to get to the bottom of Patience's disappearance.

"So when was the last time you saw her?"

Mrs. Mary had to think about that, and the fact that she was playing with her daughter's life by not contacting the authorities made the thought process harder. And then, "The day she got that strange call."

"Who was it?"

"Someone name Christine."

His mind racing a mile a minute, Capri wondered how Christine got Patience's number. Judging by the look on his face, Mrs. Mary got the feeling he knew who the caller was. "Name ring a bell?" she asked, also noticing the stain on his sleeve and putting that in her mental Rolodex.

Caught between a rock and a hard place, he had a side to choose, something that'd never been a problem until now. Certain Christine couldn't hurt a fly, he lied, said, "Nah. I don't. But I'ma call Tameko, see if she does."

"They hell with calling her, she works at Foodtown on Linden Street.

"I'm on it!"

"You got an hour. If nothing comes up, I'm calling my

husband.

"Aiight, I'm out."

Outside he called Christine. While the phone rang, he pulled alongside Zest, told him, "Them niggas got Patience."

"What niggas???"

"Hold on," Capri said having got an answer. "Christine there?"

"Hold on."

Moments later, Christine said, "The baby's kicking again, boo."

Capri hating doing this, but he knew he had no choices. Phone in one hand and the wheel in the other, he headed to the supermarket in hopes of clearing her. As he drove, out came the words, "I'ma ask you two questions, and you better tell me the fucking truth."

"About what?" she snapped.

"It's some serious shit going on, and all indications point to you. Did you call Patience? Did you see her?"

In her defense, she said, "What for? I didn't call her. And I don't even know what she looks like!"

"You said the same thing about—"

"That hoe bitch Daffany? That's it. That was different. I swear on our child, I did not call Patience. Nor did I see her! She's lying."

"Stay in the house!"

Capri was in trouble, and he knew it.

TWENTY FOUR

After being tailed for several hours, Brother Joe on his accord pulled over. But it wasn't until he arrived at the office building of his powerful attorneys.

Three white men with hard faces sporting expensive trenches and top hats were posted up outside of 11 Park Place. One of the men was waving his arms – like he was a landing instructor out on a tarmac – directing Brother Joe to park in a spot they'd reserved from him.

Four unmarked Crown Vics came to a halt boxing him in. agents converged like an offensive line, Trent picking up the rear. The tinted window of Brother Joe's Lincoln came down and out came six hands, palms up, surrendering to the many guns pointed at them. Just like that, the target of Trent's manipulated evidence was apprehended without incident.

In minutes they were face down on the asphalt being told, "Get down! Stay Down!"

While Brother Joe was being cuffed and taken into custody, the car was being searched and the other two individuals were being identified, Trent decided to introduce himself to the dapper dons whom he quickly recognized for frequenting the news and smiling with victories. They represented prominent mob figures, media darling and entertainment moguls.

Agent Atkins peeped it and raced over for a piece of the glory as Trent was saying, "FBI. Agent McCants."

"And I'm Atkins. Agent Atkins that is."

Defense attorney Rodolfo, and these are my associates, Savino and Manning."

"the make 'the case go away' firm," Trent returned. "Not his time."

"Yes, we do make cases go away," Rodolfo replied modestly, his old and red face lacking emotion due to the Botox. "I represent Mr. Abraham, and I would like to know what, if anything, he's being charged with."

Both his associates waited for the response with their thick nose pointed towards the sky. They were extraordinary in their respected fields and lived on the pages of the New York Post and Daily News.

"Hey you, take it easy over there with my client!" Manning, a portly cat in his late 40s demanded, when he saw a Timberland in the back of his paycheck.

"Which one is your client?" Trent retorted.

"All three of them," Rodolfo said smiling and revealing a mouth full of coffee stained teeth, which temporarily took the attention from his huge red nose. "What are the charges, I ask again?"

"We want Abraham for two homicides. And that's just for starters."

"My I see the indictment?" asked Rodolfo, his wrinkled hand extended.

Just as Trent was setting the stage for the arrest, some nondescript agent announced, "Add gun possession to ." he was holding six automatic handguns. "The serial numbers have been defaced."

"Like I said, the homicides are just for starters," Trent stammered walking towards Brother Joe. "This is the part of my job I love so fucking much. Joseph Abraham, you're being charged with the murders of Franc Locket and Brandon Banks."

"What?" barked Brother Joe looking to his longtime attorneys.

"Joe, just relax. We'll handle this. Trust me," warned

Savino, the stud of the trio.

"You have the right to remain silent, anything you say can and will be used against you," -Trent looked to Rodolfo – "you have the tight to an attorney."

"You can't be serious???" Brother Joe lamented. He was uptight, and started writhing. "I don't know these dudes!"

""Most murderers for hire rarely do," Agent Atkins inserted.

"Hey McCants" another agent shouted, "We have some bodily fluids in the trunk."

"DNA!" Trent replied, feeling himself. "Maybe it belongs to the victim of some unsolved murder."

"That ain't my fucking car!" Brother Joe screeched.

Loc E Loc didn't like that, felt like Brother Joe was talking a little too much to be an experienced gangster. Baby Blue thought of Patience, she being the last person they trunked.

"Joe, be quiet! We'll meet you at the precinct." That as Rodolfo and he was furious. "Manning, get the limo ready!"

The tow truck pulled up, the culprits were stuffed in separate cars and hauled off to 250 West 135th Street.

"Savino, I want you to het Mr. Outen on the phone. Let him know we haven't been retained to represent the other two niggers. Then pull up everything you can on that goddamn McCants. I want everything from the day he was born to his plans for the future."

"I'm on it," replied Savino, best known for forcing crooked cops into early retirements.

"And when you're done with that, call Judge Dropenski and see if he can get us a bail tonight. I'm supposed to be playing golf with him this weekend. Me, him and two pretty brown whores."

250 West 135 Street
7:50 P.M.

All three men were fingerprinted, their mug shot were taken, then Brother Joe was tossed in a holding pin. Two other assisting agents marched Loc E Loc and Baby Blue into a cell adjacent to the one Brother Joe was pacing.

"Yo, officer!" Brother Joe called out.

"What?"

"Tell Agent McCants I wanna talk to him!"

"This better be important," the officer replied/

Once the gate keeper was gone, Brother Joe hollered down the tier, "Y'all niggas keep ya mouth shut! You hear me!"

"What???" Loc E Loc snapped, uptight about the fact that they were nabbed by the feds and they hadn't even put no real work in on them slobs yet. "You keep your mouth shut!" he added, on some real cocky shit.

"What?"

"You heard what the fuck I said!" Loc E Loc made clear.

"Nigga is you crazy?! You better watch ya fuckin' mouth, young boy, before—"

"Before you what? Nigga, you washed up. You and ya man Action. He can't even control his daughter, and them slobs got y'all niggas losing sleep."

Brother Joe was vexed and the fact that Loc E Loc may've been right just added more venom to it. There was no telling if he'd ever see the streets again, or if he get off, how long it would be before his case was brought before a jury. As he tried taming his thinker, he heard Loc E Loc telling Baby Blue, "They sent for us."

Blue replied, "You tripping, cuz. We need them to get us out of here. Remember, I got that drama back the way. And if it's that girl's DNA in the trunk, we done cuz. I hear the Bloods is running the state pins out here."

"Brother Joe!" Loc E Loc called out.

"Yo?"

"That's my bad, just a lil' frustrated. I ain't never been pinched by the feds. Dig me?"

"Don't worry about it. Be cool, and we'll be good," Brother Joe returned, again pacing.

Trent McCants came strolling down the tier feeling real good about himself. The only thing lying between him making love to his wife and a good night sleep was Jackson's input and Moe B Dick fingering Joe in a lineup. "Didn't Rodolf, oh I mean Rodolfo tell you not to speak to me," he said.

"I was just wondering if you were related to the McCants up in Yonkers," Brother Joe poked, almost certain it was his daughter they were holding captive.

Baby Blue and Loc R Loc listened wondering what the fuck Brother Joe was thinking.

Trent said, "What's it to you?"

"Just curious."

Trent peeked back over his shoulder, saw the coast was clear, said, "Give me two million and I'll see to it, one of them west coast jokers take the fall."

Brother Joe was appalled, but at the same time wondered if this cat was serious or pulling his leg. But what he did know was, there's no price on freedom, and the easiest way to beat a case in the beginning, so he thought long and hard before looking Trent in his green eyes and saying, "You jiving?"

"Think about it, and if you send for me again, I'll know you know I'm serious."

When Trent got back to the front desk Agent Jackson and Brother Joe's trio of lawyers was present.

"McCants, we need to have a word," Jackson stated, then walked off indicating Trent should follow him.

Upstairs, Agent Jackson said, "We got a problem. Those three men in the Italian suites represent some of the wealthiest people in the Tri-state. I got my promotion because Savino made the guy before me resign at 45."

"I know who they are!" Trent snapped tired of Jackson's slick mouth.

"I'm just saying! Right now I want you to get downtown, there's a girl there with two broken legs, a broken arm and a whole lot of information! Get down there now! I'll handle this."

TWENTY FIVE

"**S**omething ain't right," Capri began. "Mrs. Mary said Christine called Patience. But Christine saying that ain't the case."

"So more or less, somebody played the oky-doke on Christine?" Stink shouted over Zest.

"More or less. Follow me!"

He sped off, caught a string of lights leading him out the outskirts of Yonkers and into the city, before running into congestion. The traffic before him could barely move, still he hit his horn. Time was slipping away. And as he removed his eyes from his watch he noticed the blood stain on his sleeve. Wondered had Mrs. Mary noticed it.

"Move this fucking shit!" he shouted out the sunroof. As soon as he got the slightest space he wheeled up on the sidewalk and sped down Broadway. Zest right behind him. The worst that could happen was someone walking out of a shop. He didn't give two shits at that moment.

At the end of the strip he found an open intersection and took that straight to Foodtown. Capri got rid of the jacket then headed inside with 32 minutes to learn something.

There was Tameko, working the 10 items or less isle. And from where Capri stood, it appeared as though time was against him. At least ten restless shoppers were lined up.

"Tameko!"

She looked up to see Capri looking real stocky in a thermal.

She then noticed his cohorts, one she wouldn't mind meeting, and the other she knew. She said, "I get off in ten minutes!"

"I'm pressed for time. I only need two minutes, if that."

The busy supermarket had fallen silent. Shoppers, baggers, and other cashiers looked on like he was about to drop to one knee and propose. The manager made himself seen, whispered something to the mocha dime piece. She nodded, then removed her smock making room for the manager to take over. In the dairy section, she said. "Dude only gave me two minutes, Pri. What up Savon? Long time no see?"

"Stacking this paper," Zest said matter-of-factly. "Holla at Pri. And it's Zest, baby."

This smile emerged on Tameko's face that let it be known Zest had made her day. "Pri, what up?"

Capri said, "Patience is missing."

"Missing how?"

"Nobody knows where she is."

"The last time I spoke to her she was suppose to be meeting some chick name Princess in Manhattan."

Zest's jaw dropped.

Stink said, "There it is!"

"Come on we out!" Capri spat, heading for the exit.

"Zest – wait!" Tameko murmured. "Here."

She scribbled her number down, put it in his hand, said, "Call me. And I hope y'all find out what's up with my girl."

"I will," he returned. Two minutes later he was in a race to Central Park West. The Henry Hudson Parkway belonged to them. They were going so fast, they nearly missed the West End exit. But somehow both cars managed to make the sharp turn. When they got up to the apartment, they didn't knock, they barged in. to find Princess laying on her back, breathless, face covered in blood. Half her right hand was at the other end of the table she had to've be sitting at.

"Ooooohh – shit!" Stink bellowed at the sight of her severed conditions. Her blouse was shredded. Revealing her massively

207

bruised tits. Her lips were swelled so bad, it looked like a bad case of injections. And her ears were leaking blood.

Zest was taken aback. Of all the violence he'd administered or witnessed, this was by far the worse.

Capri checked her pulse hoping she wasn't dead yet, and sighed one of relief when she moved. "She's still alive." He then looked around, made an observation. "Look at the paper scattered everywhere. Paper bag and cash. Princess, can you hear me???"

"Somebody tried to blow her ass up!" Zest realized.

"Exactly. Whoever gave her the money had explosives attached that would activate upon the removal of one of the bands."

"Like the shit that blows up on money stolen in bank robberies?" Stink clarified.

"Yeah. And they tried to kill her fucking ass! Princess, who did this to you?"

"Pri, she can't hear you!" Stink told him.

She glared through her nearly closed eyes, found the strength to pronounce, "I'm sorry. Action has Patience."

Capri snatched a cushion form the sofa, put it to Princess' face and smothered her ass, kept the pressure on until she stopped struggling. Zest watched with mixed feelings. Thinking of when it was all so simple, and then wishing he'd had the guts to do that weeks ago.

Downstairs, Capri said, "It's time to play my wild card!"

TWENTY SIX

"It's a miracle she's alive," a nurse told Trent McCants after checking his credentials.

"Did she speak to anyone?"

"She refused."

Trent waited until the plump nurse in the bright scrubs was done talking then he slid inside. Lying there was a lovely young lady, twisted like a voodoo doll. He wondered what'd happened, who'd beaten her, exactly what she knew, and how it was connected to his case. She initiated things with, "I'm Drew Hamilton. In the last few months I lost my sister, murdered. My boyfriend, murdered. This kid I was fucking with just got killed tonight. And I was nearly killed.

"Who are you?"

"Tyanna Jenkins."

"Shyann's sister?"

Tyanna nodded.

"I'm working that case."

"I know that's why I asked for you. And I know I'm no saint, but I don't think I deserve to die."

Trent moved a little closer, saw the fear in her eyes, as well as the larceny. "Do you know for a fact who's behind the murders?"

"I can give names and dates going back to 1991."

Trent's heartbeat doubled. He was about to take a seat, prepare to take her statement, when his phone rang. "Be right back."

In a quiet hallway of Bellevue Hospital, he answered, and the first thing he hears is. "Your witness is dead."

"What witness?"

"Mo B. Dick!"

"What?" Trent muttered, his face as long as a disgustingly hot day.

"The one who fingered Abraham! Maurice Burke!"

"How?"

"His lady slit his throat."

"Nah," Trent sighed.

"Yes! She in custody! And Abraham's about to walk!"

"But what about the guns, the DNA???"

"One of the California guys are taking all the guns since he's wanted in Los Angeles for multiple murders. The DNA – nothing there. He walks. Him and the other fellow."

The halls began to spin.

"McCants!"

"Yeah?"

"Savino said to let you know you're done! And you know what?"

"What?"

"I believe him. And guess what?"

"What???"

"I'm not going down with you!"

As the line went dead, something had come over Trent. Instinct told him to call back, but instead he slid back into the room. He let Tyanna spill her guts. Took notes while deciding his next move. He had enough to put Action, Brother Joe, Capri and his entire crew away for life. Underground at ADX. He couldn't believe this eighteen year old knew so much, was so close. Made him think about his daughter, and exactly what she knew.

"Anything else?"

"Yeah. Action's daughter was with Capri tonight."

"When he tried to kill you?"

"She was shooting at me," Tyanna cried.

Trent rested his index finger on his temple, tried to make sense of this. "I thought you said Capri and Action were warring?"

"They are."

"But his daughter was with Capri?"

"Yes!"

"Shooting at you?"

"Yes!"

"She's hanging out with her father's enemy?"

"I heard through the grapevine that Action is responsible for the murders of his moms and pops."

"Did you tell this to anyone else?"

Tyanna said, "Not yet."

At that moment Trent decided he'd heard enough.

"Wait, where are you going?" Tyanna grimaced.

Trent took the elevator downstairs, made sure he was seen leaving the hospital, then took the back stairs back up. Tyanna never saw what was coming.

Back at the prescient things were quiet. All business. Rodolfo, Savino, and Manning stood around like statues, their powerful presence resonating loud. Everyone involved with the apprehension had a long face, disappointment seeping into their souls. Brother Joe and Loc E Loc walking out, side by side, hurt their pride. Atkins wanted to put bullets in them and deal with the repercussions, that's how bad it hurt. Loc E Loc was so caught up in the hype that he wasn't thinking his man may never see the streets again, or watching the crooked eye on him.

Right outside the precinct was a champagne Taurus, keys in it, courtesy of Action. Brother Joe thanked his attorneys, then got comfy in the car. Loc E Loc did the same. They rode for a while, nowhere in particular, just to see if they were being followed. Certain they weren't Brother Joe pulled over at liquor store, told Loc E Loc, "Go grab us a bottle of champagne."

"Don't leave me, cuz," Loc E Loc grinned taking the crispy c-note from Brother Joe's hand.

"I ain't going nowhere, trust me," Brother Joe assured him. When Loc E Loc departed the car Brother Joe picked up a note he'd noticed.

It read: As soon as you get a chance all me! The Voice.

Loc E Loc returned with a magnum of Moet, and two plastic champagne glasses, told Joe, "Now all we need is some of that chronic."

Brother Joe pulled off looking for a pay phone. When he got to a stoplight, Loc E Loc handed him the bottle thinking it would be inconsiderate to pop it on another man's dollar. Joe didn't pop it though. Once he got to a secluded area, no eyes on them, he bashed Loc E Loc in the face with the bottle. The impact of the first swing sent his nose bone upward into his brain.

"Don't you ever in your fucking life, talk, to, me, like you ain't, got no, sense!" Brother Joe roared, continuously bashing Loc's head in with the weapon of choice. He then leaned over Loc, opened the passenger door and kicked the body out behind the bus terminal. "Stupid muthafucka!"

TWENTY SEVEN

The trembling wouldn't stop. Patience was terrified, cold and alone, locked away in some dark, dark garage where she'd been held for days. The swelling on the right side of her face had gone down, but the gash on the inside of her mouth was still wide open. She was famished as well, having not eaten in days. And her sweats and panties were soiled with urine, the result of a suddenly weak bladder. On top of that, she couldn't see anything and could hear very little. Her only way of keeping her sanity was to believe God would see her through this.

Every time she heard something she'd rush to the door, put her ear to it. One voice stood out. The first time she heard it she'd answered Capri's phone. While she sat, her mind wandering, she heard footsteps, the voice, both getting closer and closer. She scooted to the door, put her ear to it.

"How the fuck???"

"I don't know daddy. I was on 125th and he jumped out, put a gun to my head. Give him what he wants! Whatever it is."

Capri snatched the phone, said, "Mines for yours!"

Action glared at the bolted door jailing Patience, devastated by the latest news and hot it would corrupt his plans.

"One hour, 147th Street, bus depot behind Esplanade Gardens. Just you and Patience! Or you never see your daughter again!"

"My daughter better be there, and not a hair on her head

213

harmed!"

"Man, put Patience on the phone!"

"How did it come to this Capri?"

"I thought you'da figured it out by now. You think I started picking your mans off for nothing???"

Patience heard the footsteps again, the bolts move. She retreated to the far wall, got low and pulled her knees to her chest. When the door opened there stood the man with the acerbic voice, no mask. He had on a black Peacoat, black jeans and boots, a black kufi on his head.

"Say something!" he ordered Patience.

"Help me!" she shouted.

"Patience!" Capri shouted back.

"Mines for yours!" Action spat expecting that call from Brother Joe any minute. "Mine for yours,' he repeated, before hanging up.

Brother Joe never did call Action. Instead, he called the one soldier he knew he had left. Man-Man.

Man-Man was up in some skins when he heard his Cellular. Sweat dripping from his forehead, he rolled out of her snatch reaching for his jeans. "Who this?" he bellowed, breathing heavily.

"B.J., nigga. I want you to meet me on 125th by the Westside Highway, right now bee."

"Why, what up?" Man-Man began, before adding, "I heard you got bagged."

"Well, I'm out. Remember that fifteen grand I gave you?"

"Yeah!" Man-Man replied, his girth and length vanishing.

"Well, it's time to start earning it! I'm on 125th right now! It's a whole lot more money involved."

"I'm on my way." Man-Man hung up and got dressed.

"Where you going?"

"None of your fuckin' business, Daffany. Just be naked when I get back, laying right there just like you are right now!" he sneered, his eyes all over her round tits and that wet puss between her brown thighs.

"I went through this with my baby father before he got killed. You think I'ma go through this with you, you bugging!"

"Shut up! I be right back!"

Ten minutes later Man-Man was exiting the Westside Highway on 125th Street. Without delay he spotted Brother Joe with his swat cap pulled low, army jacket zipped up tight, that gold toothpick sticking out the side of his mouth. He pulled up alongside him and hit the horn. Brother Joe gestured for him to move over – Man-Man did – and Brother Joe got in.

"Where we going?"

"Queens," Brother Joe seethed, veering into traffic.

"Queens?"

"Ain't that what I said?"

Man-Man leaned back and went for the ride. It was a quiet one that lasted thirty minutes. He couldn't his eyes. They were pulling up to a brick and stone mansion spanning hundreds of feet from end to end, several stories high, and had more cars in the driveway than necessary. He knew it didn't belong to Brother Joe when he pulled a gun as they crept around back.

Man-Man asked, "Who lives here?"

Brother Joe pulled another gun. "Here. And don't worry about that. Just shoot if you have to. Drenae may be an introvert, but the bitch is vicious too."

Brother Joe was there for the money, his windfall. The millions Action kept stashed there in case of a ransom, or if he had to flee the country on short notice. He knew exactly where it was, and exactly what he was going to do with it. Only, somebody else was there packing it into huge duffels. As they were rounding the rear of the home, they heard voices coming from inside. Voices they couldn't make out.

"This shit is heavy, boo," Katrina whispered.

"Stop bitching, and come on. Two more bags, and we out. In and out without being detected."

"Then what?" she asked, still unable to digest the fact that she was robbing her family for a nigga she wasn't even sure she'd be with.

"We gotta go meet your father," he whispered back, remembering the promise he made to Mrs. Mary.

Katrina wanted to shoot back out to Miami where she got her cherry popped, and make love to her man until she was too hungry to move. To sore to walk. To thirsty to talk. Simpering, she got back to work.

The bags were heavy, so stuffed, that they were dragging them. Dragging them to the side door, which was about ten feet from the back door. The first two trips, when they got to the door, Capri tossed the straps over his shoulders and hurried them to the van. They had one more trip to make. But things took a turn for the worse.

Capri spotted Brother Joe as he was exiting and backed back inside. And then Man-Man in the shadows. "What the fuck?" he queried, shocked by the discovery. Their eyes locked as Capri dropped the bags and pulled his automatic. Man-Man saw the glisten of the nickel plate, and reached for the gun Brother Joe had given him, only to find out the clip was empty/ at that moment he wished he'd never been infected by envy, but it was too late. Capri was backing down. Brother Joe was swift, but Man-Man wasn't so lucky. He was sent flying backwards, meeting the dumpster with two gaping holes in the chest, and a, "You bird ass nigga!"

Katrina, in panic mode, grabbed the duffels and scurried the opposite way, towards the van while Capri engaged in battle with Brother Joe. Slugs were flying, and all Drenae could do was wonder what was going on below her. While racing A.J.to their panic room, the shots stop. Then started back up. Once inside, the door secured, she could hear nothing.

Below her lay two wounded men, one still clutching his pistol the other trying to remove the space that'd come between him and his pistol. Blaka!

Katrina's eyes lit up when she seen Capri emerge, and then

she saw the blood. "Baby, you're shot."

"Get in the van and drive. I'm good!"

Katrina reached out to touch him, and he barked, "I said drive!"

While she drove, he tied his flag around his bicep. The bleeding slowed, but the time didn't. "Pull over!"

"I got it," she replied, rolling her eyes and pressing harder on the gas pedal.

His phone rang. And that's the only reason he didn't slap her and take the wheel. "Yizzo."

"Son-in-law!"

"Trent? How you get this number?"

"My wife."

Capri paused. "So you know?"

"No. I don't. but what I do know is if you want to stay out of jail, and help raise that baby your side chick's carrying, you better meet me right now."

"What side chick?" asked Capri baffled.

"Trina! Now do I have your attention?"

Capri's world stopped moving for a second. "I can't."

"Yes you can."

"I can't!"

"Why not?"

"You really don't know?"

"I guess I don't."

"But you know about Christine?'

"Tyanna's alive. So I know a whole lot more!"

"What???" Capri panicked.

"She's in the back seat of my car with two broken legs. Says you killed some dude on Fifth Ave, and that you tried to kill her."

"And what she want?"

"It's more like, what I want."

"And what is that?"

"A pension plan since I blew mine trying to help you."

"What you mean???"

"I have a witness willing to cooperate in the back seat of my car."

Another pause. "147th between Seventh and Lenox."

"What's over there?"

"Me, I'll be there."

The line went dead.

"Pull over!"

Capri got behind the wheel and rode into his destiny. He didn't stop thinking until the bus depot was in sight. Until Action was visible. Until Patience saw him, the gun in his hand, the nape of Katrina's neck in his other.

"Mine for your!" Action barked, the nozzle of a Uzi in Patience's lower back. "You all right, babygirl?"

"I'm good, daddy," Katrina purred, unable to hold back her urge to grin. She'd dreamt of this day, the look on his face when he realized he'd been played, ever since he slapped her.

"Patience, you good?" Capri called out.

"I just wanna go home!" Patience bemoaned.

The only way anyone would go home was if Trent saw him drive by as he'd planned. That's exactly what had happened. And Trent lost it when he spun the corner and saw his daughter hemmed up. Once a marksman, he took aim. But at the very same time he squeezed, his daughter made a run for it. That missed shot ignited a mess. Capri sent shells at Action who hit the deck and threw some back. Patience running for safety, took one to the stomach. As she collapsed, falling to the pavement, Capri turned on Katrina, splattered her mask. Trent couldn't believe his eyes how cold Capri really was, and never saw Action sizing him up. Action now had a cop killing on his hands, but he'd never face a judge or a jury. The loneliness, the hurt, the anger of growing up without parents is what drove Capri. Had him charging with the voracity of a wild cat, squeezing with each step. By the time he was up on Action, there were so many holes in his face and neck, Capri just stated towards Patience all choked up on emotions.

"Don't touch me!" she gasped, clutching her midsection, and ignoring the tears in his eyes.

"Come on," he begged. "The hospital's not far from here."

"I said, don't touch me. You're a murderer!"

"Come on. I can't leave you here, like that ma. Love you too much," Capri reasoned over the sound of sirens in the background.

"Love ain't what you say," she sulked, propping herself up, "it what you do."

After trying to corral Patience once more and being rejected again, Capri mounted the van. He circled the block, red and blue lights in the distance. There it was. The Crown Vic. Tyanna stretched out across the back seat.

"Hey, you!"

Tyanna peered up.

Blaka! Blaka! Blaka!

EPILOGUE

The only survivor of the bus depot massacre, which made the front page of the New York Daily News, claimed she didn't remember anything. Who kidnapped her, who shot her, or why. She claimed she didn't even know her father was there, or that he'd been murdered. Told them she'd never met, or seen Tyanna Jenkins, Princess Quinones, Joseph "Brother" Abraham, Anwar "Action" Outen, Katrina Outen, or Markeef "Man-Man" Peacock – all which were gunned down the same night she was nearly killed. And was very convincing when questioned by investigators. Didn't even flinch when asked, "What about Capri Hayward? When was the last time you saw him?"

She said, "It had to be before it got cold. So, the summer."

When nothing made sense, the FBI released a statement claiming Trent McCants was a rouge agent acting on his own accord, and that he didn't die in the line of duty. It went on to say, "The day he was murdered it'd been brought to our attention that he was selling information to an undisclosed network, compromising an investigation that is still ongoing. Out of greed."

A few weeks after the FBI released that statement Capri was picked up at Harlem Hospital for questioning in multiple murders while awaiting the birth of his first child. He never left the 'hood, tough he did purchase a nice piece of property in Hoboken Hills, New Jersey. After pleading the fifth and requesting counsel, he was arrested on gun charges. About a week later two indictments were handed down for the murders of a twenty year old stripper from Queens, and Derrick "Destro" Rowe. He was held without bail, and remanded to Rikers Island to stand trial.

The first missive he sent out was to Patience. She never responded. Never visited. But he did receive a card from her mother wishing him well and thanking him for keeping his promise. It came from Alberta, Canada, where she and Patience decided to start over.

Christine assumed the role of wifey, and didn't get big headed when Capri told her, "I got six mil' in a wall at the Jersey spot." However, she did go from a bad ass project chick to prominent socialite on the New York scene. His daughter, whom they appropriately named Olivia, had the best of everything, as well as two godfathers.

Zest went on to become New York's 90's era Fritz, the consignment king. Capri and Stink remained his silent partners, while Lanky and Wildlife blew up serving as his capos. He even started moving like the old legend becoming an avid traveler and major playboy with the women. But that didn't last long. He eventually fell hard for Tameko and relocated out to Hoboken Hills,

Stink and Rosa never did make it to Hedonism, but they did tie the knot. The reception was held at the Jacob Javits Center, with more than 100 guest on hand. After their ten day honeymoon in the South of France, where they spent half their time on a yacht in the Mediterranean Sea, he held the grand opening of Stink's Audio. His very first legitimate venture. A car dealership quickly followed. Things were good, but the limp, was a constant reminder of a failed mission.

After the vigorous advocating of one of Stink's newest associates, a city councilman, Marcel Sr. was transferred to a state prison on Staten island. There he dedicated his time to the worship of Allah and teaching Orthodox Islam, hoping his Lord would forgive him for slaying Will Bill in the name of the almighty dollar.

Iris left the coke alone, and Queens for Harlem. But Capri, she would never leave. She remained loyal, communicating via mail, calls and occasional visits. No other man was able to fascinate or captivate her the way he had, which is why she had no problem sacrificing her life and liberty making sure he didn't lose his.

Because Capri's crew understood that friendship wasn't an opportunity, but a responsibility, prosecutors decided to put a plea on the table. One that would make Capri eligible for parole in the fall of 2004.

As for Action's old lady and young son, unforeseen foreclosures forced them out the min mansion and into a homeless shelter.

And the beat goes on!

ABOUT THE ARUTHOR

On this one, I wasn't really thinking about the critics or commercial success, as was the case with my first two novels. (RESPECT THE STRUGGLE and STREET GENERALS) My goal was to move the readers, the ones fiending for that rush of excitement only found in the streets. That had me deeply devoted to developing and bringing depth and truth to each character. Dedicated to creating a compelling story line that would be truly unpredictable. More decadence, more drama more villains.

Even though this book is deeply rooted in crime, and defies the expectation and conventions of society, I think a lot can be learned from it. I don't expect to win an NAACP Image Award, but I expect to be taken serious as a writer. I expect to expand vocabularies and broaden perspectives. With each novel, I'm still learning as I go, which is amazing, and it resonates in the work. Parts of this book was written at work, but most of it in traffic. There's so much more to come. I feel like a little—known star staring to shine. No Grind, No shine.

Made in United States
North Haven, CT
23 April 2022